Singapore at Home

"A rare glimpse behind the politely but firmly closed doors of the Singaporean heartland, distinguished by its gathering of resident voices across nationalities, ethnicities and creeds."

—Alvin Pang
PhD, Poet & Editor
2005 Young Artist of the Year (Literature),
National Arts Council Singapore
2007 Singapore Youth Award (Arts & Culture)

"Home, leaving or buying a home, familial politics and ambivalences, poignant complexities of migrant and diasporic experiences, sanguine to ironic reflections on that interface between home and self-identity—these stories pack a punch by unpacking familiar themes through intimate scenes and surprising scenarios, regularly hitting too close to home. Stripping away the gloss of the quotidian and the everyday, the narratives welcome the reader like a passing voyeur into the residences of characters pacing corridors of the self while interrogating the manifold meanings of home and relationship."

—Cyril Wong
PhD, Poet & Fictionist

"What a delightful mix of stories about home, homecoming, homing in on distances that build and separate us."

—Felix Cheong
Poet and 2000 Young Artist Award (Literature),
National Arts Council Singapore

Singapore at Home
Life across Lines

Editors

Pallavi Narayan
Iman Fahim Hameed

Kitaab
Singapore

KITAAB

First published by Kitaab,
an imprint of Kitaab International Pte Ltd
10 Anson Road, #27-15, International Plaza,
Singapore 079903

Kitaab International
Singapore

ISBN: 978-981-14-8045-4

Printed and Bound in Singapore

www.kitaabinternational.com

To all my friends who made Singapore home for me

Pallavi

To Imran, Isa and my family

Iman

And when we turn within the cage
Our bodies make, and find a sea
With neither tide nor age,
An act of bonding sets us free.

—Edwin Thumboo
in "Evening," from *A Third Map:
New and Selected Poems* (1993)

Contents

III. Precarity and Tenacity

IV: Home and Away

Introduction

Pallavi Narayan & Iman Fahim Hameed

The thought of home is imbued with bliss and pain, comfort and guilt. In all its manifestations—whether it moulds us or breaks us—home nurtures a tender, heart-breaking beauty. A lived space, it shapes our life experience. But more importantly, the people we share our home(s) with transform the meaning we seek in a place that is hopefully our refuge. In *Singapore at Home: Life across Lines*, we ask what constitutes 'home' in Singapore. In a country of seeming impermanence and blink-and-it-changes scenarios, what kinds of homes do, or have, we lived in? And what are the gender relations within these spaces? Where are we overlapping, bridging or overriding boundaries, biting our tongue to keep silent, losing our cool, being triggered, being cherished? In noticing that which is transient, do we miss out on what *is* permanent—the relationships that make rooms and houses into homes? The well-worn spaces of the home can both maintain and subvert gendered notions. Do they uplift all genders' dreams or border on the edge of a nightmare? What are those lines that are drawn so restrictively in our minds? Can we overstep them now and then at the risk of upsetting the status quo? Does that collection of rooms we name 'home' quietly absorb gendered meaning? In our conversations and actions with those who make up our family, what are those unnamed feelings that we battle with in our heads? Or is it, conversely, here that we find our rest?

In its assertion of the importance of community in an altered perspective of living and being in the home, this anthology attempts to claim Singapore's domestic and social spaces anew through the medium of short stories. Our contributors explore their worlds through a combination of personal narrative and fictionalised incident. It is commonly known, however, that fiction is usually grounded in truth. But the real world and the reality of relationships can sometimes make us feel stuck or scared, or unable to portray with exactitude what lies deep in our hearts. In our attempt to bring stories of home together in this book, we sought therefore to protect identities where our contributors saw fit, in an attempt to grant grace and a sense of freedom in their writing. We believe we have succeeded to a good measure. In the stories that follow, readers will be treated to a diversity of voices that Singaporean homes clamour with—from settled generations to immigrants to migrants, to those who stopped here long enough to make it their home for a while. In the COVID-19 situation the world was thrust into since 2020, we have been spending much of our time at home. But do we find this a welcoming situation or something to tolerate, or instead a predicament that pushes us to the brink of circumstances that we are only yet beginning to decipher?

Singapore at Home: Life across Lines thus calls for an urgent reflection on everyday life in the island-state, on the pleasures and frustrations that the word 'home' embodies. In it we present a variety of short fiction— real-life stories in a fictionalised format, a reimagining of gender within the home, how home can come with gendered undertones, and our contributors' interpretations of questions that we are all seeking a resolution to. More specifically, the anthology aims to explore the complexities of negotiating the modern 'outside' and obsolete 'inside', and the strategies we use to deal with the dilemmas and conflicts they give emergence to. This compilation is an empowering space for the collective and tilts the axial search for identity, no matter what gender we are.

Singapore's culture has always been marked by language; ironically, language also gives rise to certain narratives that gain dominance, pushing community accounts to the periphery. Here we then see stories from disparate cultures and countries of origin, all of which are on location in the city-state and deal with its peculiar predicaments and charms. English writing in Singapore happens to be that curious thing that has metamorphosed into a sort of canon. Our colonial past has imbued us with manifold ways of approaching English(es). Indeed, English has been shaped to the intonations of Singapore's other national languages—Mandarin, Malay and Tamil— and patois, and we encouraged our contributors to use local phrases and dialects, as well as versions of English that are in interaction with nationalities from around the world. While being immersed in, and emerging from, a distinctly local scenario, the book appeals to a wider, more global audience as it expresses local community concerns around gender in social and familial spaces in the cosmopolitan city-state. Ultimately, we are seeking here to unravel some of the problematics surrounding the concept of gender as it functions in Singapore.

Individuals and communities have changed the rules and norms that maintained gendered roles on the outside, but have they succeeded within? Are we perpetuating the same stereotypes by projecting strength as masculinity? Are we fleeing from the spaces that define gender, and by doing so, maintain that very definition within those spaces? The stories here engage with such questions and extend the exploration of how the space of home can both subvert and maintain gendered notions. In their minute detailing of the spaces in and around the home, they reflect the country's everyday—from migrant homes to more settled 'locals' in their own unique realities. Our attempt is to show that diversity not only helps us negotiate social spaces and the private self, but universalises the shared confusions of genders and spaces in Singapore.

In their accounts, the contributors emerge from HDB flats, condominiums, shophouses and landed estates alike. As the narrative shifts from one kind of residence to another, the milieu around the characters also changes. To take nature as a metaphor—from boxed-in plants in HDB complexes to the landscaped gardens of expensive condominiums to the small balconies and doorsteps of shophouses that nurture pots of bonsais to veritable wildernesses of flowers that erupt around landed estates—the stories flow through an abandon of emotions. These are tightly braided into tales which are nuanced and relatable, inviting readers, through their taut words, to let their senses flow. As indeed home life is bound in spoken and unspoken rules and schedules yet offers flexibility and moments of tranquility, the writing, in its precision, entices readers to dwell a while, perhaps over a cup of tea, and reflect on their own memories. In our submission call we asked for a strong plot, interesting character development, tightly drawn scenes and gripping dialogue; the stories that follow are the ones that grasped our attention, either striking us immediately as just right for this volume or, on the other hand, alluring us with a lingering evocation of enchantment or intrigue. We took some time to get back to all those who submitted their stories for a reason, and it was this—that we wished to wait a little and see which tales, accounts, portraits and sketches stayed with us, divulging another layer of meaning on rereading.

The volume itself is a labour of love, transpiring from a writing workshop at Singlit Station that local writer Clara Chow helped organise and conduct in January 2018 towards the event Ungender Home, and where Pallavi gave critical feedback to participants while also writing. In July 2018, Ungender Home, a conversation conceptualised, produced and co-hosted by Iman under the collaborative Katha, was held at Aliwal Arts Centre, where some of the attendees of the earlier workshop, including Pallavi, read their works, artists exhibited their paintings and classical Indian dancers interpreted a poem written by Iman. The discussion following this well-attended occasion gave impetus to the conceptualisation of this collection and while we invited our colleagues at the Aliwal event to submit their writing for consideration, we opened up the call for everyone who had ever had any connection with Singapore. After significant deliberation, the stories we finally selected are those which tread a fine line between delicacy and firmness, balance and teetering a little over the edge. They encapsulate, within their hold, sentiments that stop just short of boiling over with passion, intensity marked with delicacy, ardour tempered with warmth, softness enhanced with fire, coldness iced over with loneliness, solitude alleviated by company, anger and frustration signifying grief—instinctive reactions, gut feelings and premeditated responses, exhibiting all along portrayals of spirit and resilience. The characters—who may be placed along the full spectrum of intuition and rationality—appear from living rooms, bedrooms and bathrooms, kitchens and pantries from a plethora of apartments in blocks towering into the sky to generous properties that betoken a leisurely pace of living. Together they await the MRT at the concourse or platforms along the various lines, alight from buses, zip around in cabs, board aeroplanes to and from distant lands—creating, keeping, breaking homes as they proceed on their life journey. Hence we have introduced loose sections in this anthology to hint at the possible routes the stories take as they bring us into their heart and hearth—into what each contributor perceives as the meaning of home.

And how ever can home ever be complete without friends and family traipsing up and down its familiar paths? In Section 1: Neighbours and Relatives, then, we are privy to the most confidential secrets of the various members of the family, with mixed undertones. 'Her Father's Business' by Ken Lye has us sitting down to what is, to all appearances, a cosy family dinner in celebration of the daughter Ling's good grades. The jocularity surrounding the generous helpings of steamed grouper, sweet and sour pork and the plethora of dishes is, however, laced with ominous implications. This spectacular and shocking first story of the book, set in Geylang, is finely and tensely wrought. In 'The Pushover' by Clara Mok, we take a hurried, purposeful walk with Madam Hong, who is visiting her son and daughter-in-law in their spacious HDB flat. As we wearily climb up the stairs and trip down in her company, stopping briefly for a *kopi* with old acquaintances, we witness a hidden-in-plain-sight view of Singapore with a surprise ending. Anna Onni, in 'Potted in Place', gives us a tragicomic take on neighbours on corresponding floors of an HDB block. The relationship between Amelia and her neighbour's boy Valerian, that buds over plants, abounds in loneliness and neglect, and is simultaneously sad and amusing. A child's perspective is brought forth in a painful and exacting manner by Cecilia Mahendran in 'Merdeka'. In a complexly layered intergenerational storyline that follows Singapore's history, Mahendran portrays the lives of three young women dealing with the penetration of the outside, here male, world into their space. This leads us nicely to 'Papaji's Desire', Surinder Kaur's account of Daljit, freshly returned from Toronto, who must now grapple with her mother's attempts at arranging her a suitor. Kaur takes us through the frustrations of a modern woman navigating dutiful love and the pains of traditional expectations while delighting us with a refreshing father-daughter bond. The section concludes with 'Home without Walls' by Phyllis Wong—a reprise on a solitary existence through the life of Mei Chan, whose home overwhelms her with reminders of her parents and siblings. The story shows us how she seeks to make peace with her aloneness in the community.

But why be despondent when unlikely allies as well as treasured intimates alike are waiting in the wings with reassurance and fellow feeling? Section 2: Comfort and

Sustenance captivates with just such compassionate and serene tales that are simultaneously tearful as well as joyous. We rise at dawn with the birds in the restful 'The Gardeners of Lim Tai See' by Aparna Das Sadhukhan, in the house of Jhumpa, a newly wedded young lady who is also fresh to Singapore shores. Unemployed and with no company, Jhumpa is invited to harvest flowers and herbs with Aunty Chia, with whom she nurtures an unexpected warm friendship. As they explore Singapore together in buses and on foot, Jhumpa inexplicably starts feeling more secure in herself, until tragedy strikes. 'Memsahib' by Ranjani Rao is a straightforward appraisal of the settling in of a woman into Singapore as she embarks on a second marriage and the challenge of creating a new family with hers and her new husband's children. In a pointed contemplation of the events of her life leading up to her carving a new identity, Rao's narrator finds herself relying, to a large extent, on her Filipino help whom she likens to the sisterhood of female figures that she grew up with. Kalpana Mohan, in 'A Room of Our Own', reminisces about her visits to Singapore, which she considers a second home. She brings us right inside the familial relationships that she holds most dear, complete with affectionate anecdotes, sensitively and humorously describing the complicities of sharing a room in a condominium apartment in Tanjong Rhu. 'Aaji's Vicissitudes' by Payal Morankar is a fond rendition of a visiting grandmother attempting to understand and fit into the, to her eyes, alien lifestyle of her granddaughter, right in the middle of the COVID-19 curfew and the furore over stocking up from the supermarket. In 'Roses', Ilya Katrinnada Binte Zubaidi introduces us to Malay customs and traditions in a nostalgic, elegantly rendered family portrayal told from the perspective of a child, that centres around a family visit to the grandmother's grave in a cemetery. Investing us into the tiniest details, she paints them as the most exquisite in the interplay of shared recollections.

From the collective to the individual, Section 3: Precarity and Tenacity turns the spotlight on those who are in a daily battle of survival in the city, and find themselves grappling with odds and obstacles that are particular to their situation. 'November Hope' by Rolinda Onates Española is recounted in the first person, landing us straight into the dormitories of female migrant domestic workers from the Philippines, Indonesia and India, who are awaiting pick-up by their employers. Onates Española's matter-of-fact, no-nonsense manner and stark description underlines the desperation that shrouds every encounter. In 'Knock Knock! Who's There?: Work from Home Stranger', Anjali Patil gives us the internal monologue of a female domestic help established in the fancy, but small, condominium flat of a couple who attempt to negotiate the unanticipated time spent both working and living at home during the pandemic. Audrey Tay, in 'Maid in Singapore', shows how a house help, in surmounting commercial and emotional challenges, fights to amass and remit enough finances to her home country to build something of value for her family. In so doing, she is overcome with a wave of sentimentality and pride. In 'The Pangolin' by Euginia Tan, the distinct depiction of theatricality intermixed with loneliness is cast in crisp images. The fear of the ageing man, desolate in his hidden identity, is brought out vividly in the confines of the bedroom, but the search for absolution is far from complete. Rejection finds a unique voice in Gargi Mehra's 'No Place for Loneliness'. Ritesh, the new corporate arrival in Singapore, realises that the golden ticket comes with no friends, no hangouts and no niche that he fits into, until he is hit out of the blue with a startling proposition.

Criss-crossing into Section 4: Home and Away, we are led into the unknown realm of personal growth as characters evolve and articulate, at first with reluctant hesitation and then with empowered confidence, the metamorphosis of the concept of home for them as they themselves alter. In Dia Feng-Lowe's 'Rock', Moira attempts to come to terms with her role as expat housewife in a new city, and her faltering confidence is confused with ill-placed affections. Isha B., in 'Rediscovering the Familiar', inspects the emotional conflict coupled with the relief of homecoming from foreign shores. The decision to return home permanently, not only to one's country of origin but also to the familial domestic space, is tinged with anticipation that settles into an annoyance with the familiar. 'A Bold Crossover: (The ABC of a New Beginning)' by Azeena Badarudeen is an assertion of the self, of moving away, if only a little, from what the narrator has known—the area of Toa Payoh and its corresponding MRT line. We see the protagonist Alyna wrestling with the dilemma of leaving the past behind. Mason, in 'Locomoting' by Vanessa Ng Q.R., is the itinerant wanderer who now feels a craving for stability in a new place. But will he be able to remain grounded? The last story of this section as well of the anthology wraps up the connecting strands of all the stories in its warm grasp. 'Arriving' by Arathi Devandran immerses us in the home and its environs—its losses, its gains, its everyday loveliness. The narrator, who stays, moves out, leaves, creates new homes and new families and returns to stay only to depart once again. What Devandran meditates on is not only the yearning of a maturing narrator but also an empathetic glance at other family members.

The anthology provides a rich tapestry of life in our most private space. When read in its entirety, the numerous threads that run through this anthology, weaving the stories together, become evident. And while the overarching subject is home, the narratives inadvertently involve work and its relation to the home, whether for instance it is Ling's father's shop in Geylang ('Her Father's Business'), Mason's travel-intensive job ('Locomoting'), jobs that bring immigrants like Ritesh to Singapore ('No Place for Loneliness') or homes that became places of work, for example, for Nenek ('Roses') or Melina ('Knock Knock! Who's There?: Work from Home Stranger'). Prior to leaving for work and on returning home, the responsibilities are numerous. The stories also then delineate the varied tasks that are divided amongst the members of the household ('Rock') and leave us debating on whether roles such as cleaning, cooking or dropping the kids to school ('Memsahib', 'A Room of Our Own') or running a shop, fall into a gendered delegation of roles or are divided equally amongst the family ('Merdeka', 'Home Without Walls'). Who takes care of meals and packing lunches, those who are ill and elderly, paying the bills and arranging for long-term life plans? Are traditions carried through forcibly and as a compulsion of societal pressures or do new customs topple power dynamics? The narratives, rich in their detailing of the everyday, shed light on some of these arrangements and how they are configured.

The many states of being bound to another—marital, filial, parental, collegial, neighbourly—as well as the sense of enforced privacy, insulation or confinement they can engender figure in many of the stories, sometimes solely as the kinship frame upon which the story hangs while at other times they become drivers of change, new beginnings and liberation ('A Bold Crossover: [The ABC of a New Beginning]', 'Aaji's Vicissitudes', 'Arriving'). These stories explore, too, separation and reunion, death, solitude and companionship—the very dualities of life. While parts of the stories can cast a somewhat dark shadow on home life, home is, after all, coloured in shades of grey. Thus shame, neglect, abandonment, mistreatment and exploitation ('Potted in Place', 'The Pangolin') and a range of subtler tensions find their way into these accounts but they are, finally, redemptive and redolent with hope, compassion and understanding between spouses, partners, mothers, fathers, daughters, sons, siblings, grandparents, neighbours, acquaintances, colleagues, flatmates, friends and the larger community. The stories together form a mosaic of the unspoken complexities of home life that is never fully revealed to most people on the outside. Perhaps one of the more important aspects of this book is the unification of migrant and local experiences of home and family ('November Hope', 'Maid in Singapore'). Placemaking, heartache, trauma, dreams and desires are universal experiences in all the stories: the returned Singaporean at odds with their old world shares the same anxiety of identity crisis and Proustian moments just as much as the newly arrived immigrant, as they both find ways to make meaning of old and new, past and present ('Rediscovering the Familiar', 'The Gardeners of Lim Tai See').

While the anthology offers diverse representation of gendered experiences of the home, it is perhaps telling that the predominant authorial voices—and several of the protagonists—are female. The characters in this collection are strong, vulnerable, flawed, unwavering in their determination and, at times, perpetuators of the very gendered norms that they themselves were subjected to. Mother-daughter tensions are rife, male privilege and gender inequality is well represented and redemptive men play positive roles in some stories. A few of the stories also explore the questions of men who grapple with and upend masculinity norms or do not give in to prevailing conventions. Papaji supports Daljit's choices—whether they involve keeping her hair short or navigating the single life ('Papaji's Desire'); Ling's brother is quietly supportive of her education and gentle with her dreams ('Her Father's Business'); Ben dotes on his wife ('The Pushover'); the brother-in-law folds the laundry and cooks *dosa* as par for the course ('A Room of Our Own'); and the husband contacts a therapist to deal with his marital woes ('Knock Knock! Who's There: Work from Home Stranger').

Homes, while seemingly permanent, are intrinsically temporal and reflect the dynamism of the individuals who live in them, which each story deals with in its own way. Some offer an exploration of linear time and how it affects attachment and meaning between the past, present and future while others take us through cyclic and rhythmic temporality and how this shifts the interpretation of home. What distinguishes a home from a house is the interaction of individuals with space and the relationships to and within them over various kinds of time. The anthology cuts across these lines to embody what home can mean to different people in Singapore. Read in sections, at random or in its entirety, *Singapore at Home: Life Across Lines* ultimately presents to you perspectives that you will embrace and relate to, and rethink the spaces in that most intimate place—your home.

I

Neighbours and Friends

1

Her Father's Business

Ken Lye

'Wait until everything is ready,' Ling's mother said in Cantonese as she emerged from the kitchen with her daughter's favourite dish, steamed grouper with shallots and ginger. She placed the plate on the lacquered surface of the table, the grey-marbled fish in its bath of salty sauce staring open-mouthed at the girl. Already served were beef with black beans, sweet and sour pork, and crunchy spring rolls. With the inevitable dish of stir-fried vegetables and large bowl of pork marrow soup with peanuts and lotus still to come, Ling wondered how everything was going to fit on the dining table.

The reason for the elaborate dinner: a clean sweep of A1s and A2s for Ling's O-level examinations. She would be the first in her family to go to junior college. Not one of the fancy, elite JCs, but the important thing was that she had managed to avoid the polytechnic route that her elder brother Seng had taken. She was still on track to achieve her ultimate goal of studying at a foreign university. It was unlikely that her parents could afford to pay for an overseas education, running as they did only a humble claypot rice eating house at the end of a row of derelict shophouses in Geylang. But Mrs De Silva, the school's guidance counsellor, had helped Ling map out a path to a potential scholarship. Ling had been a prefect at Northshore Secondary as well as captain of the girls' badminton team—and she was committed to working hard to achieve a sterling extracurricular activity record in JC as well.

'One of you call your father!' her mother said, slapping Seng's hand away from the chicken wings. 'It's so late, and he's still not home!'

Mrs Wan wiped the beads of sweat off her forehead then doubled back to the kitchen. Ling's brother drummed out a steady beat on the edge of the table with his chopsticks as his gaze returned to the television set across the living room of the family's three-bedroom HDB flat.

'Oi, call him!' Ling urged, kicking Seng's foot.

'You call, *lah*!' her Dai Gor[1] replied. On the screen, Singapore Broadcasting Corporation star Huang Yi Liang soared into the air to engage in a sword fight with a ragtag team of martial artists.

'I'm the guest of honour tonight! How come I still have to do everything?'

'You think you go A-levels, big deal *ah*?'

Seng brandished his chopsticks like weapons and pouted mockingly at her, his lower lip mashed against the upper one. Then he broke into a goofy grin and crawled out of his seat.

'Anyway, this show is shit,' he said, as he dragged himself to the phone by the side of the television. On the way over he messed up his sister's hair, ruffling it playfully with his right hand as if rubbing a dog's belly.

'I just washed my hair, you ass!' she said, smoothing her hair down and pulling it back into a ponytail with a scrunchie. He was such a pain, but she would miss him

---

[1] Big Brother.

4

when he graduated from poly later in the year and left home for National Service. Most boys she knew dreaded going into the army, but Seng was different. He had been in the National Cadet Corps in secondary school, and still went back to help train the current cohort in rifle drills. The army was a chance to relive his glory days before having to find a job, settle down.

1992, it seemed, was going to be a milestone year, the start of big life changes for both of them.

Seng put down the phone and turned the television set off.

'No one is picking up,' he announced in Cantonese, and in his loudest voice, so his mother could hear him.

'Must be on his way back!' came the reply, a disembodied voice from the kitchen over a rousing thunderstorm of pops and sizzles as hot oil drew water from fresh *kai lan*.

Just then they heard the shuffling of feet, shoes being kicked off, the scraping of a key at the door. Mr Wan, a gaunt figure of a man, had barely made it through the threshold when his wife began her attack with a shrill 'Why are you so late?'

'It's okay, Ma,' Ling sighed. 'Let's just have a peaceful dinner.'

Mrs Wan carried out the soup, her hands bundled up in Good Morning handtowels. She glared at her husband but held her tongue. Without being asked, Ling went into the kitchen to bring out the vegetables, rice and small soup bowls, while Mr Wan removed his sweat-stained t-shirt and slumped into his chair at the head of the table. The obligatory chant of 'Pa, Ma, eat,' and then dinner began. No one said another word as chopsticks jabbed at the plates of food, and soup spoons plunged deep into the container of fragrant, porky broth to reach the treasures beneath the surface. A home-cooked dinner wasn't exactly Jack's Place or Swensen's where Ling's friends had celebrated their good grades with their families, feasting on steak or fish and chips, but her mother was an excellent cook, and this was a lavish spread by any measure.

Ling relaxed. Theirs had never been a talkative family. Meals were functional, the necessary prelude to everyone sitting around the television: father and son first, mother and daughter joining in after the washing up was completed. They would bring with them a plate of cut fruit—a few slices of apples or oranges for all of them to share. The one time that Ling had visited a classmate for dinner, she was amazed (and a little envious) at how much conversation the family engaged in: what did you do at school, what are you up to this weekend? They talked as if they were all friends having a meal together after school at a McDonald's. Ling nearly choked on her food when Esther's parents asked the girls about their thoughts on what was in the news. Ling's parents probably didn't even know the name of the JC she was going to, much less her opinion on the recent chewing-gum ban.

As Ling's mother reached over for a piece of the grouper, however, Ling heard her grumble under her breath: 'I don't know what is wrong with some people. Your own daughter has done our family proud, yet you cannot even be bothered to come home on time.'

Mr Wan brought his bowl of rice down from his mouth.

'I'm working at the shop, bringing home money to feed this family. What more do you want from me?'

'Ma, Pa ...' Ling tried. Beside her, Seng continued his meal as if the quarrel were just noise from the television set.

'I don't go out drinking and gambling, and still you want to complain?'

'Work, work, work, but it's not as if we are living in some rich man's mansion!' Mrs Wan grumbled as she placed a chunk of fish onto Seng's plate.

'Stop buying such expensive food all the time! You think I am the Emperor of China?' he said through a shower of saliva and a few specks of half-chewed rice.

'This is a special occasion. Your daughter—'

'My daughter? What is there to celebrate?'

Ling had always suspected his feelings on the topic. Easier, however, to just never allow herself to think too hard about it.

'So, what if she can go on to A-levels and university? She is just a girl. She is going to get married out of the family anyway.'

She hoped he would stop there, but he continued: 'Don't waste the money. Better to keep for Seng. He is the one taking over the shop.'

Her father was being particularly belligerent this evening though Ling did not know why. He should be used to her mother's nagging by now, she thought. The woman's provocations were no more pointed than normal. Ling looked over at Seng who remained preoccupied, carefully removing the needle-like bones from the fish in front of him.

'I can also take over the shop what,' she said, half to herself as she pushed a stalk of *kai lan* around in her bowl.

Her parents fell silent.

'It's not like Dai Gor even wants to—'

'Don't bring me into this,' Seng interjected in English, one hand raised pointedly at his sister.

She turned to her father, and continued in Cantonese: 'The place automatically goes to him?'

'Of course,' her father replied. 'Everything. The flat, the shop, whatever money I have left. Whoever heard of the daughter inheriting the father's business?'

'I don't matter at all?' She didn't want the eating house. She didn't want his money, but she could not accept the straightforward manner in which her father was now speaking. Her throat was bone-dry, her eyes hot.

'Alright, alright, forget I opened my mouth,' her mother said quickly. 'It's all my fault. Let's just continue eating.'

'Why is the whole family talking about money tonight? I'm the man of the house. I'm the one who earns the money, so I decide who the money goes to.'

'It's not your business. It's Ma's.'

Ling felt a hand on the edge of her elbow.

'Hey!' Seng warned in English, but she was on the brink of tears now. This was supposed to be a celebration.

'What did you say?' her father asked.

'Who wants the stupid shop anyway? So hot and dirty. Doesn't even have air-con.' I would never take my friends there, she wanted to add, but before she could, he rose to his feet, yanked her out of her chair by her shoulders with one hand and slapped her across the face

8

with the other. His whole body was trembling with rage, but his hand was steady and sure. She had never seen her father so angry before but, of course, it was because she knew the right words to cut into him most deeply. She was her father's daughter, after all.

'Are you crazy?' her mother screamed. Seng got up and tried to pull his father's arm down. He was bigger, but the older man showed surprising strength and kept his arm raised. They knocked into the table as they struggled. Plates were thrown off-balance, emptying themselves of their sauces and gravies, the soup bowl barely holding in its contents. A porcelain spoon fell off the table, and chipped as it hit the floor.

Ling stared at her father.

'I hate you,' she cried and then, with one hand pressed against her cheek, she ran into her room.

Seng knocked at her door an hour later and let himself in. Ling was in bed, a blanket pulled up over her body, the fan blasting cool air directly into her face. The room was dark, lit only by the glow of the corridor lights outside her window. Her brother planted himself down, his heft unsettling the mattress, so that she bobbed up as if on the crest of a small wave.

'Still angry?' he asked.

She flipped over so that she looked directly at the wall.

'I know you are also unhappy with me, but whatever I said wouldn't have made a difference. He's not going to change his thinking.'

He spoke in whispers which she wondered about until a light waft of cigarette smoke drifted in through her window. Her father was smoking in the corridor again.

'So, I have to just accept it? After all the hard work I put in. And for what?' she said to the *Xiao Ding Dang*[2] stickers on the wall.

'Because you're smart. Smarter than your dumb older brother who nearly didn't even make it through Normal stream.'

'I only did better because I studied. Anyway, it's not like I even made it to a top-five JC.'

'Whatever it is, you're going to make something of yourself. You could get a job with the government or at a big-shot multinational company, even run your own business with some fancy marketing degree.'

'Pa doesn't think so.' She reached out with a finger and scratched at the corner of one of the stickers Seng had stuck up on the wall many years ago. The siblings had shared this room as kids until their grandfather had passed away. Then Seng had moved into their Gong Gong's bedroom, and this one had become hers.

Seng sighed, then continued: 'If I tell you something, you must promise not to tell Ma I told you.'

She was intrigued, but still mad at her brother for not sticking up for her. She kept her back to him and continued working on the sticker with the nail of her index finger in the dim light.

'Today's the last day of the month. Yi Ma always comes over to our place.'

Ling was not aware of this, but she did know that her father had never liked her mother's only sibling. Her

---

[2] Doraemon.

mother's older sister had married a wealthy entrepreneur with a chain of electronics stores all over Asia. With his money, she had started her own successful business, a gift shop selling upmarket hampers on Orchard Road with a snooty French name. Their family lived in a huge bungalow along Bukit Timah Road, and were always going on holiday to far-flung places like Europe and America, while the furthest Ling's family had ever gone was Genting Highlands in Malaysia. Yi Ma had been very happy to have nothing to do with the relic of an eating house that Ling's grandparents had instead passed down to their younger daughter. Or rather, words unspoken, their son-in-law. At that time Ling's father was a few years out of secondary school, and doing odd jobs.

'She comes in the morning when we are all in school. She says it is to see Ma but really, it is to give Pa a cheque. I don't know how much.'

Ling felt her heart close in on itself.

'The shop used to do well but in the last few years, business has been bad. If not for Yi Ma, Pa would have had to shut the place down long ago.'

Just when she thought Seng had finished speaking, he added: 'It's not easy for him to take her money, you know?'

Her Dai Gor raised himself off the mattress. As he was leaving, he stopped by the door where Ling had left some sports equipment leaning against a bookshelf. Out the corner of her eye, she could see him bend down to pick up a badminton racket.

'This is mine,' he said. He pressed against the strings with his wrist once, twice, checking the tension. The net across the head held.

'Take good care of it,' he said, putting the racket down.

Ling sighed. She was acutely aware that she would soon have to crawl out from under her blanket and make her way to the corridor to apologise to her father. Get down on her knees if she had to. It was still her fault, even if it wasn't. But not yet. For now, Ling lay in bed, breathing in her father's cigarette smoke, as she continued to tear away at the stubborn edges of her brother's old stickers.

2

The Pushover

Clara Mok

'You know *ah*, I'm here at Ben's for the fourth time this week,' Madam Hong lamented. Her underarm skin flapped about loosely on her arms as she strained to mop the floor of her son's five-room Housing and Development Board (HDB) flat.

'*Pai Mia!*[1] Sixty years old, still have to do this!' she sighed. Her jade bangle clanged onto the handle of the mop as she stretched to clean underneath the sofa. Her arthritis sent a bolt of pain which attacked her knees and she winced.

'Cat! Don't sleep here. Go to the kitchen. Go! Go! Go!' she urged, prodding her daughter-in-law's white feline with her mop. It was curled up with its bushy tail tucked in, refusing to move.

'Waa! This cat *ah*, like she's the queen or what *ah*.'

Earlier that morning, Madam Hong was at the wet market to pick up some fresh fish. She passed by her four old neighbours seated around a table at a coffeeshop and they waved her to an empty seat, 'Madam Hong, join us for coffee.'

'Today cannot *lah*, got to go and help my son,' she replied.

'Go and help your son for what?'

---

[1] Wretched life (lamentation).

'Help them sweep, sweep, mop, mop *lor*.'

Loud gasps could be heard. 'Why spoil them?'

'Never mind *lah*.'

'They don't have hands and feet *meh*?'

'My own flesh *mah*. Don't want my son to be so *jialat*.[2] After work still got to do housework, cook ...'

'Your *sim pu*[3] *lei*?'

She leaned close and whispered in a conspiratorial tone, 'My *sim pu*, J-lyn, Ee-lyn, don't know what Lyn, I call her Mei Lian. She's so lazy, never help out at all. Always on her phone and laptop. Some marketing manager, so what? Think she's some big shot, *aiyoh*, refuse to iron his clothes. What to do? I iron for him *lor*. So *sim tia*!'[4]

Clucks of disapproval echoed around the table.

'This is how she speaks.' Madam Hong cleared her throat and spoke in a seductive manner, 'Good morning, J-lyn speaking. Mr Tan, how may I help you?'

Her dramatised act sent her neighbours into stitches. 'Why is she like that?' asked one.

'She's from a rich family. Got maid. Good thing she gives me some pocket money. She brings out her handbag, super expensive one, got one V. Yes, MV. Purse also MV.' She cleared her throat and spoke in her mock-demure voice, 'Mah, here's $50 for you, go buy yourself something nice to eat.'

---

[2] To be in a bad shape.

[3] Daughter-in-law.

[4] Heartache.

Madam Hong took a deep breath. 'I want to tell her, nowadays, $50 where got enough to buy anything? The *ngoh herr*[5] I buy is already how much?'

'Don't help them, ask them get their own part-time cleaner,' another suggested.

'Cleaners charge $10 per hour. One week I go there ten hours, is $50 enough? Nowadays, cleaners where got easy to find? Some very dirty, some steal things, *aiyah*, must well I do *lor*. Not difficult what. Just that I am getting old. Knees go creak, creak, creak! Cannot bend down to scrub the toilet, back pain!'

A wave of sympathy washed over her neighbours. 'What about your son?'

'My son *ah*,' said Madam Hong, her smile widening. 'That day, he took the mop from me. Go, go, go, go sit in front of the TV, let me finish up here for you. My heart was like, wow, so happy, you know. My only son, carry nine months in my stomach. Not bad, eh? He asked me *lim kopi* and even steamed my favourite *ang ku kueh*[6] for me to eat. *Woah*, better than winning Toto!'

A faint glow of crimson shone on Madam Hong's angular face before it folded into a grimace. 'Then I ask him. Today Tuesday. Why come back so early? Guess what? He says, got retrenched. *Gek sim!*[7] Company bankrupt! *Aiyoh*, my son, so *jialat*.'

Revelling in the rapt attention showered upon her, she continued, 'I don't understand why my life is so hard. My first husband, he died at twenty-seven. Loan sharks

---

[5] Threadfin fish.
[6] Red tortoise cake shaped to look like tortoise shell with fillings like sweet mung bean or peanuts.
[7] Heartache.

came after us for money. My second, the *si lang tao*,[8] lucky he died already. See, my bruises. After so many years, still like that.'

'Madam Hong, don't think about the past anymore. All the bad things happen already. *Guan yin niang niang*[9] will give you a good life.'

'I don't dare think about it. That day at *Si Beh Lou*,[10] you know, I pray to *guan yin niang niang*! You give me a bad life, never mind, now give me a good death!'

A flurry of hand gestures of frantic dismissal followed. '*Choy! Choy! Choy!* Why you talk about death. Not scared, *meh*?'

'Scared for what? Everyone has to die.'

'But you've no grandchildren yet!'

'*Aiyoh*, I may not have the *hock kee*.[11] My son wants to wait a few more years.'

Madam Hong bade her neighbours goodbye and tottered towards the bus stop. She armed herself like a female general going to war. Cradled in her arm were a few plastic bags, one of which contained a thick slice of *ngoh herr*. In another was a cleaning cloth, known for its extraordinary absorbency bought from a makeshift store.

'Mah, you're here,' greeted Ben, as he unlocked the door and ushered Madam Hong in. She held a duplicate key to their flat but on Sundays she remembered to ring the doorbell.

---

[8] Curse word: dead people's head.

[9] Goddess of Mercy.

[10] Waterloo Street, Singapore, where the famous Kuan Im Thong Hood Cho Temple is.

[11] Fortune.

'Mah,' Jacqueline said, looking up from her laptop for nary a second, her mobile phone cradled at her neck. She carried her laptop into her study room and left the door partially open. Her lipstick-stained mug lay on the coffee table, her prized cat perched nonchalantly on one of the pillows strewn on the floor. Ben headed for the kitchen and a sniff of her favourite *ang ku kueh* drew a churn in her empty stomach.

Madam Hong removed the plastic wrapper of the absorbent cloth and started to clean the table, shaking her head at the ill-placed mug. She lifted up a long black strand of hair and dropped it with disgust. *So much hair! Now there's even white ones.* She lifted a piece of white fur and dropped it into the bin with flourish. *The house is full of black and white hair. Does she bother? No lah! Continue to yak, yak, yak on the phone.* Through the open door of Jacqueline's bedroom, she could hear her voice.

'Darling, come rub my back for me. So sore after I sat the whole day working on my laptop,' cooed Jacqueline.

'Sure, babe!' replied Ben.

Rushing from the kitchen where he was washing the dishes, he grabbed a bottle of lemongrass oil from the cabinet. Then he positioned himself next to Jacqueline as his hands kneaded through Jacqueline's tough neck muscles down to her back. All the while, Jacqueline was lying face down, eyes closed.

Madam Hong kept shaking her head as she watched this incredulous scene unfold before her. To her utter disbelief, Ben unclasped his wife's bra before spattering her back with oil and spreading it evenly across her back with his skilful fingers. *When did my son become like that? Didn't he play rugby in school? Where has his manliness gone to?*

17

She blurted out in a fit of frustration, 'Hey, son, I want to talk to you.'

Ben replied, 'Mah, I'll be out in a minute.'

Leaving the door ajar, Ben stepped out of the room and spoke to Madam Hong at the door.

'Son, you call yourself a man? No shame? Rubbing your wife's back after removing her bra. Earlier I saw you scrubbing her underwear in the washbasin. How disgraceful! *Aiyoh,* it's bad luck, *sway.* Don't you know that's the reason you cannot find a job?' said Madam Hong, her lips quivering and her hands fiddling with her jade bangle.

'Mah, I love my wife and will do anything for her. She will also look after me. You will, right, babe?' Ben said.

Jacqueline's voice rang out, 'Yes, darling. Come massage again. It's sooooo good.'

Madam Hong gave Jacqueline a dagger stare. Then she marched out of the flat, cursing under her breath for the umpteenth time. 'I'll never step into his house again.'

I cannot stand living so long and watching my son becoming toufu.[12]

The vibrancy of Toa Payoh was a great welcome as she walked down the stairs into the street. The multitude of people and the old shophouses dissolved in the background as she remembered the bygone days of her second marriage.

Wang's feet rested on the coffee table, his grotesque paunch protruding like a pregnant woman's in her final

---

[12] Beancurd. When used to describe a person, it means that the person is weak-willed and soft.

month of pregnancy, his chin glued to the horse-racing pages of the evening newspapers.

'Ah Huay! What are you doing?' Wang shouted.

Madam Hong replied, 'Cooking dinner ...'

'Stop that useless work! Come and massage my aching body. I work so hard and no thank you from you!' Wang hollered.

She wiped her hands dry on her apron and knelt down beside the couch where he lay without his shirt. Madam Hong grimaced as the muscles on her lean arms strained from holding on at two-second intervals but he kept saying, 'Useless woman, press harder!'

'Faster!' he yelled, rolling up the newspaper to smack her head. She cringed, not daring to make a sound, her hands kneading nonstop.

'So slow!' He kicked her stomach with his legs. She squirmed like a wounded cat, which had the effect of provoking a fresh wave of fury in Wang. Picking up a porcelain teacup, he smashed it on her head.

Many times Madam Hong stood at the kitchen window, her red-streaked eyes surveying the height and impact. 'If I jump down, what will happen to my son? My poor son, no one to take care. *Sway*, want to die also cannot.'

In a show of defiance, she spit into Wang's tea. The act gave her a moment of superiority, an act of defiance which brought about giddy pleasure. Her fear was betrayed by the trembling of her lips as she served tea to her husband. Luckily, she maintained a straight face throughout.

When Madam Hong was a young girl, her mother clucked when she examined the mole under her eye.

She said, 'Huay *ah*, your life is full of trials, *pai mia*.' The multiple crosses along her life line on her palm foretold the predetermined tumultuous life she was born into and she accepted her fate without questioning it.

After ten torturous years together, Wang passed away from a heart attack and she rejoiced in her self-concocted mark of liberation. In contrast to her earlier cropped short hair, she now wore her tresses long and flowing. Wang had refused to let her grow her hair in the past and his frequent hair pulling had resulted in a bald patch on her scalp, coyly hidden below a faded khaki hat. With her savings she bought some coconut oil, massaging it into her scalp twice a day. Her relatives remarked that her countenance was rosier than ever and exuded so much charm that it was hard to believe that she was a second-time widow.

She ignored those remarks, toiling day and night just to support Ben through his education. Besides washing clothes for households, she took up various odd jobs to make ends meet. Finally, her hard work paid off and a smile radiated from her face when she posed with Ben in a studio photoshoot, a university scroll clutched in his hands.

Madam Hong sniffed, dipping her fingers into her bag to search frantically. Squinting at the display of her mobile phone, she attempted to muffle her sobs. When she had calmed down enough, she answered the call.

'Mah, it's me.'

'What is it?' came her curt reply.

'Err … Mah, don't be angry, okay? If you don't want me to wash Jacqueline's undies, I won't do it …'

'You young people have your way of thinking, your way of doing things.'

'Come on, forgive us, Mah,' cajoled Ben. 'I made your favourite *ang ku kueh*.'

'*Mmmpf! Gek sim ah!*'

'Come on, Mah!'

'You go and take care of your wife. Don't need to care about me,' Madam Hong said as she choked up. 'I can take care of myself.'

'Where are you, Mah? I come and find you!'

'At Block 32.'

'You stay there, I come over.'

With a plastic bag of *ang ku kueh* in his hands, Ben searched for the slightly bent figure of Madam Hong and spotted her seated at a circular table at the void deck. 'Mah, here's your *ang ku kueh*.'

Madam Hong removed the squarish piece of banana leaf and tucked into the *ang ku kueh*. The crunchiness of freshly pounded nuts with a thin layer of glutinous flour whetted her appetite.

Later on, she would remember to narrate to her neighbours, 'Don't call me soft-hearted. I forgive my son but not my *sim pu*, listen carefully ah. My son asked me to go to his house again, say what J-lyn wants to say sorry. I believed him.'

Madam Hong followed Ben up to his flat. The walk took a toll on her and she drew heavy breaths. Her knees clicked like a machine needing oiling. She shuffled behind Ben, her footsteps heavy.

Ben's face drained of colour when Jacqueline ran out of the flat, tears streaming down her face. He moved away from Madam Hong and hugged Jacqueline, soothing her, 'Jacqueline, what's wrong?'

Jacqueline pouted and pointed her manicured finger at Madam Hong. 'Snowball's dead! It must be Mah! She fed something to Snowball.'

An air of indignation rose up in Madam Hong. 'Don't anyhow say *hor*. It's your cat. I didn't feed your cat anything. She's like a queen sitting there in the living room and I just do my mopping.' Seeing Ben's eyes darting between his wife and her, she added, 'Ben, believe me.'

'Hush! Hush! Don't cry, darling. Did you call the vet?' Ben asked, his eyes soft. Jacqueline nodded and burst into tears once more.

'Mah, you go back first. Let me handle this.' Ben said. Shoulders sagged, he motioned Madam Hong to go. *What? She climbed all the way up and was asked to go home* liddat? *Now the cat die, also her fault. Her life cannot compare to a cat's.* Gek sim ah!

Madam Hong dropped one leg after the other, clutching to the railing for support, her knees sending bolts of pain into her body with each step of stairs she took. She paused to recover and catch her breath before she headed towards the coffeeshop for respite.

On a normal day, she would order *kopi siu dai* or less sugar at the coffeeshop. That day, she asked for the thickest version possible of the coffee, *kopi gao*. Madam Hong sat in a remote corner of the coffeeshop, her thoughts in a turmoil. She swirled the forbidden richness in her mouth before letting the thick beverage slide down her throat. *Hack the high blood sugar. Anyway, if she dies faster, also nobody cares. Someone once told her, having a kid is like that.* Gek sim! *Nobody tells her, when they grow up, it hurts harder than before.*

Madam Hong's thoughts turned to the time when Ben was born. When she looked into her newborn's eyes, she felt like she was so lucky. *But now he's grown up, see* lah, *what happens? Wife comes first. Everything is darling this, darling that. What about his old mother?* She shook her head and sighed. *Old* oredi. *Live so long for what? Torture herself only.* She took another long gulp of her *kopi gao*.

She shuffled out of the *kopitiam*, her mind entangled in an ominous cycle of thoughts, blinding her senses. A speeding motorcyclist heading towards her direction as she stepped onto the road.

When her eyelids flickered open, her legs were in a cast. A growing dread overwhelmed her. *How she wished that* guan yin niang niang *had fulfilled her wish to die. Why was she still alive?*

'Mah, Mah! You're awake,' said Ben.

'What happened to my legs?' asked Madam Hong.

'Mah! A motorcyclist knocked into you and …'

'And what?' insisted Madam Hong, her chest tight.

'The doctor says you cannot walk anymore.'

The news hit Madam Hong like a bolt from Heaven. *Previously, having weak legs was bad enough. Now she could not walk. How was she going to carrying out simple tasks like easing herself?*

On the day of her discharge, Jacqueline pushed Madam Hong in a wheelchair, a thin piece of cloth covering the cast. 'Mah, I'm sorry to blame Snowball's death on you. Forgive me, Mah. Come and stay with us. We'll take care of you,' Jacqueline said.

Madam Hong wrestled with the myriad of emotions tugging at her. *Trouble my son and sim pu?* The past accusation in Jacqueline's eyes replayed in her mind.

Repeated attempts to halt the vicious replay of events before she crossed the road that fateful day failed. What if they had invited her to their house again, instead of dismissing her? A series of 'what ifs' coalesced into a lump of regret that plagued her mind, plunging her into a state of depression.

Trouble her sim pu *and Ben to take care of her*? She had been helping them, not the other way round. Now that Ben was jobless, she had to depend on her *sim pu* financially. The thought made her shudder. Madam Hong insisted on staying in her own spartan two-room flat in Ang Mo Kio. 'But Mah, you need someone to look after you!' Ben pleaded.

'Well, I am old and useless,' sighed Madam Hong, punching her lifeless legs with her fists.

'Mah, stop that!' pleaded Ben, holding onto her fists and placing them against his heart. 'Give us a chance to repay you.' The regular rhythmic beat of Ben's heart had a hypnotic effect on her and eased the pressure off her fist and her heart.

It seemed that Heaven had sent a message to Madam Hong and she surrendered fully to her fate. 'Perhaps that's what *guan yin niang niang* want for me.'

3

Potted in Place

Anna Onni

'I– I– am Vah-lehr-ian.' A little boy of five appears beside her as she waters her little jungle of plants in the corridor. He stands expectantly, staring at her. Her darling herbs and gingers will have to wait. Annoyed but trying to be neighbourly, she puts the watering can down and turns to face the interloper.

'Pleased to meet you, Valerian. I am Amelia.'

'Hah-lo. Ah-meh-i-lia.'

Amelia smirks at the kindergartener's struggle with words. She finds children funny from a distance. Entertaining enough when they approach, but otherwise better kept and groomed by adults who care about that sort of thing.

'Play with me!' Little Valerian stomps his foot like a dictator-in-training.

Amelia frowns. 'Didn't your parents tell you not to talk to strangers?'

'We-e juhst became friends. Wh-e-re not strahngers anymore. Play!'

Amelia struggles to point out the flaw in his logic with child-friendly terms. She wants to say, 'Stop bothering me, you munchkin!' or 'Children are maggots, go away!' These are euphemisms for what she really wants to say.

'What do you want to play?' At least this maggot seems cute. And believes wholeheartedly that she will be a good playmate, and an instant friend. Valerian is very unlike the males in her own age group of thirty-five and close to forty. Demanding, yes. Suspicious and sexist? Not at all.

'Let's play ... fighting!'

'How do you play fighting?'

Valerian has it all planned out. He takes hold of two of her metre-long wooden stakes, and hands her a pointy end with the carelessness of a child. He fake-jabs his weapon at the very concerned Amelia.

'This isn't safe. Give me the stick.' Amelia tries to take the stake from Valerian. Indignantly defending his right to play, he begins to thrust his spear into the air.

'Wh-e-re friends! Friends play! Play!' With all the force of a vengeful warrior, he flails his spear around and knocks over Amelia's bedraggled potted mint plant. The pot crashes to the ground, spilling its guts of damp soil and exposed roots. Despite her persistent care and conscientious watering it has always looked sickly, and has never produced enough leaves for more than a pot of tea every two weeks. Perhaps the shock of dislocation would finally kill it. It lies on the ground, an innocent victim in this battle between boy and woman. Amelia stares at Valerian, her new mortal enemy, gripping the wooden stake so hard that the splinters graze and poke at her skin. She feels the urge to scream.

A slightly pudgy, heavily panting woman runs down the corridor.

'Baby! Are you hurt?' On cue, Valerian scrunches up his face and sobs uncontrollably. 'Drop that!' The boy drops his spear immediately and his mother pulls him into a crushing hug. 'What happened, baby?'

Amelia shuffles slightly closer, smiling politely but trying to sound as indignant as possible. 'He's alright. He was just playing and knocked over my plant.'

'Playing? You're the adult! How can you let a young child play with something so dangerous! He could have poked his eyes out with the stick!'

Amelia has a dozen responses ready. She wants to demand an apology, at the very least. But she just wants peace and quiet now. She uses the comeback her own mother used when she was a child. 'Why do you let him run around? Someone could just kidnap him.'

Valerian's mother picks up her baby boy and says, 'I thought I could trust the neighbours here. Clearly not. *Ph-toooi.*' She spits on the ground. Some dribble slides down her chin as she turns and marches towards the staircase with her naughty little charge.

He squirms as his mother drags him away, peeking around to give Amelia a huge grin. Amelia can't help but give him a little wave. It isn't his fault that he has an overprotective mother with dubious parenting skills. Thunder can be heard from a distance. She quietly sweeps up the broken pot shards and throws the now extremely traumatised mint plant into a bag for repotting later. But she slams the gate, locks it, slams her front door and bolts it shut.

It is not her fault that parents let their spoiled offspring wander around terrorising the neighbourhood. Children with their self-obsessed stratagems to gain attention. Parents teaching their children to be mean and selfish. They assume that everyone is going to be nice to their little princes and princesses. What kind of a name was 'Vah-leh-rian' anyway? Entitled little emperor.

The boy is a sheltered flower, ready to cower behind his mother. And the mother is big enough to cower behind.

The rain is heavy, and there's nothing else to do and nowhere to go on a Sunday afternoon. She thinks about Valerian's mother. Rapidly ageing, anxious and tired. Everything about her signalled 'mother-in-distress'. She wonders about how much housework and childcare Valerian's father does. Not much, she guesses. Amelia tenderly strokes the indoor pitcher plant that she keeps at her desk. Once upon a time she was asked by a man very much like that to live a very similar sort of life. She prefers her plants.

It starts with the smallest things. For a month after her face-off with little Valerian she finds leaves and sometimes branches torn up and left lying on the ground. Just a few each time. She tries to keep watch over her territory but she is at work most of the day. Were there less flowers on her orchid plant? Had she over-watered her cactus? Perhaps she is just imagining things.

One day, she returns home from an exhausting day of non-stop meetings to find huge puddles of water under her plant pots. The soil is all waterlogged. It could have been the rain. Did it rain that heavily? Did it rain at all?

She hides the watering can inside her house.

The next day, there is a puddle of yellow water at Amelia's door. She holds her breath as she waters the plants, fearing that more watering of the same sort has been done.

Then a still-warm piece of shit appears next to her carefully re-potted mint plant.

Amelia knows better than to complain to anyone. A few years ago a smoker used her soil as an ashtray, growing a toxic kind of forest in her already finicky herb pots. The lemon balm wilted. The basil never tasted quite right. Her parsley caught fire once. She talked to the smoker who lived five floors above and indirectly tried to get him to stop. She went on for an hour about how concerned she was about the terrible consequences of second-hand smoke on his children. He had talked about his past attempts to quit and she listened with as much empathy as possible. A day later, he started to terrorise her chilli plant with the possibility of wildfire. The grassroots leaders pleasantly smiled and told her they would look into the case. An inspector came over, minus the smile, and told her that she would be fined if she did not clear away the plants that were obstructing the corridor. Fire hazard: the new label for her precious plants.

A week later, there is a bag of rotting bananas on her doorstep. She cannot tell if it is a peace offering gone wrong, a plea for banana cake or an intentional attack. Various insects are swarming around the bag, poking their way in and gathering to enjoy the feast.

Amelia wants to make a fence. Something that clearly says: stay out and leave me alone. But it would be too unnecessarily territorial. Like she owned the corridor, when obviously the housing board didn't think so. She makes tiny protest signs that are along the lines of: 'My Land, My Rules', 'A Woman's Home is Her Own Castle', 'Get Off My Plants' Property'. She hopes that staking them into her many flourishing cactus pots will make the point.

So she continues nervously watering her plants at irregular intervals, hoping to catch the non-native serpent in her garden. She whispers reassurances to her plants before leaving for work. She cannot sleep well. It is getting too warm. The world is going mad. The news is a blur of terrible calamities, furious riots, horrible predictions in somewhere elsewhere. She refuses to follow the news, becoming an expert at nodding and shrugging and giving a vague enough statement when people at work discuss the headlines. She goes to work, returns home, tends to her plants, has her dinner and then lies on her bed hoping against hope that sleep will come soon.

For a while, nothing happens. She somewhat nervously continues her daily routine of work, home, plants, repeat. Occasionally, she sees a decisively plucked off flower or broken stem but nothing more. She makes and stakes even more tiny protest signs and hopes that that will do the trick. She can't think of anything else she can do.

Amelia is proud of her corridor garden. Some friends had given her a plant party for her thirtieth birthday. It was the birthday three weeks after her mother had passed away from cervical cancer. It was both celebratory and sombre—and everyone had agreed that dead or dying flowers would be the worst thing to fill her home with. She had once mentioned that she would love to have fresh herbs to use when making meals. It was a flippant remark born from a wistful dream. She had never thought much about the practical consideration of plant care that normally functioning adults are able to manage easily. So her friends gave her beautiful orchids and gingers and pots upon pots of fresh herbs.

But Amelia had black fingers. She also could not care very much about sustaining life. Weren't plants supposed to fend for themselves in the wild? Why should a potted plant demand so much attention? She sporadically gave them a sprinkling of water. Almost all of them died in two weeks. Then Susan had come over to check in on Amelia and seen the sorry state of the once luxuriant plants.

'You need to take care of them.'

Amelia groaned.

'Here, I'll show you.'

For a few weeks, Amelia kept up with the arduous routine of watering, trimming, clearing, sweeping and checking that Susan had put in place. Then Susan came in with new seeds to replace the dead plants. Susan set up a series of meticulously labelled germinating trays and then potted the tender seedlings as Amelia complained about how much unnecessary work went into keeping living things alive.

Reluctantly, Amelia got swept into Susan's craze with growing green things. Soon, she was borrowing manuals from the library and Google searching: 'What to do when your *ficus* is dying?' and 'How do you make hothouse potted plants flower again?' Around her, friends, even Susan, got engaged, married and pregnant. Amelia had a few boyfriends but none of them were remotely accommodating towards her anxiety over her plants when they suggested a holiday to Hokkaido or even a weekend trip to Batam. Or at least, that reason was always given as the final straw after months of trying to prune her into a more accommodating and suitably kitchen-friendly domestic girlfriend.

Amelia works hard at her desk job at an oil refinery during the day and comes back home to tend to her garden. People are difficult. Plants are easy. Plants are temperamental, but they never expect you to do much. Just the bare essentials of putting them in enough sun and giving them enough water and good soil.

The next morning her favourite plant, her Fukien tea bonsai, is in the middle of the corridor. It is still somewhat upright but its pot is cracked into jagged pieces. The leaves have been plucked out, every single one.

Amelia takes no chances. Her flat catches the afternoon sun, a bad choice which the property seller had disparagingly commented on. Amelia had firmly decided on this flat as the cheapest option available to her. It will now be a boon for the twelve corridor-blocking plants she will move into the flat. On Saturday, she will buy plant lights and a new plant rack that fits in well with her living room. On Sunday, she will move all the plants into her flat, safe at last from pesky neighbours and government regulations.

For the rest of the day, she gently re-pots the tiny tea tree. She was going to get to doing it sometime anyway. The soil was getting old and dry. Once done, she carefully snips away at the tips and rewires its branches. She will keep it on her dining table and sing to it in the evenings. Perhaps it will feel brave enough to live. She will chat to it as she eats her small dinner of home-grown basil pesto and pasta. This pitiful bonsai might need some loving attention before it dares to stretch out new leaves again.

Valerian liked Amelia's plants from the moment he saw them. He thought that Amelia's corridor looked like a great forest, and imagined himself as a great warrior tracking down a fearsome forest monster. The great trees would disguise and protect him. The shrubs would give him food to eat. But after the stick had hit and broken the pot of the plant, he could no longer imagine that the branches could be the towering trunks of trees in a deep, dark wood.

His mother told him to never, ever talk to the mean auntie who lived one floor below them. His mother often left him alone. She liked watching sappy dramas and once she was hooked, she would forget to make dinner and order in food hours later. He asked to go to the playground constantly, but she said that the other children were rough and naughty. She did not want him to learn bad manners.

Valerian did his kindergarten homework and then sat on the floor. She had not said he could not play around the corridor. She did say he could not leave the corridor. One floor below was still their block of flats. And the flight of stairs was less far away than the full length of the corridor. He liked to run downstairs when his mother was asleep. He knew how to open the door very quietly. He usually knew how to get back before the end of her nap.

He wished he had a pet. A dog would be fun. He could play catch with it and watch it play dead. But he had no pet. The other neighbours didn't like him loitering outside their flats, peering in and then running away if they saw him. He wished one of his neighbours had a dog. But all they had were plants and plants don't know how to do tricks. But the mean auntie's plants seemed different.

So he stood for hours near the plants. He liked to touch them, feeling their different textures and trying to understand the network of patterns formed by their stems, branches, leaves and petals. He would bend some of the stems backwards and watch them spring back into place. Or almost into place. Sometimes the branches broke and he hurriedly ran back home, afraid of the mean auntie. One day he could not hold his pee in and urinated at her front door. Another day it was poop.

Valerian wanted to apologise to the auntie. She wasn't so bad. He bought some very ripe bananas for her with his pocket money. He had left them there when Amelia was working overnight at the office for three straight days to meet a deadline. They were blackened and attracting fruit flies by the time she got home.

One day after school, Valerian stood at the door to his home and heard loud shouting from his home. His mother was screaming. His father was screaming. He heard things like 'dumb', 'stupid', 'idiot', 'bad' and a lot of other words he didn't know. Then he heard his name. His parents were fighting about him, he was making them fight, he was a terrible boy who made people unhappy. He started to cry, and ran as fast as he could to the auntie's plants and started plucking leaves as fast as he could from the smallest plant he could find. When the plant was completely bare, he toppled it over and enjoyed the satisfying crash of the pot against the hard concrete. Then he was scared. He ran back home and found his father sobbing in the living room. His mother was not in the flat. His father held him close and rocked back and forth, still sobbing, and all Valerian could think about was how he could never, ever tell anyone what he had done to that plant.

Weeks later, when it had been a particularly bad day at school and his parents were shouting for over an hour, he decided that he could risk going back to the plants. He went over to look at the plants and saw that all the plants were gone. Not even a leaf or twig was left. The door to the auntie's flat was closed tight-shut.

4

Merdeka

Cecilia Mahendran

1959

That sick feeling in Thenmozhi's stomach returned the minute Rajeshwari amma, her employer, walked out the front door. Thenmozhi felt completely alone in the big house, despite there still being four others. Out in the garden were her employer's three-year-old son and five-year-old daughter, chaperoned by a feeble old servant. Another elderly, cantankerous servant was tending to the plants.

Inside, Thenmozhi had just the brassware to complete before she could escape the confines of the spacious bungalow. She carefully brought all the brass pieces from the display shelves to the backyard, brought out the polish and rag from the storeroom, then tucked her faded *pavadai*[1] securely between her knees as she squatted and began to polish.

Thenmozhi wished her father had never had that road accident. With a collar at his neck and a splint on his wrist, there was no way he could carry or shift crates, boxes and sacks in Venkat mama's shop for the next few weeks.

Venkat mama was the person who had come to Mallipandi, her village in Tamil Nadu, India to source manpower for his expanding provision shop in

---

[1] Half-sari.

Singapore. Her father had gone ahead first to this new land of opportunities. When he had saved what little he could, he brought the rest of the family over, but not without first selling their land and livestock so as to afford the journey by ship. Upon their arrival, Venkat mama provided accommodation for them in one of his squalid shophouses, crammed with a larger number of families than the available number of rooms. Each family had to demarcate their turf with screens made of tattered, no-longer-wearable saris or *lungi*s.[2] All the tenants kept away from them, no thanks to her father's quarrelsome temperament.

The loss of income after his accident made the father curse his children even more. He was already frustrated with his late wife for dying at childbirth and bequeathing him the burden of raising three children aged fifteen, fourteen and six. None of them were boys. As the oldest, Thenmozhi had to take over the role of mother and housekeeper.

'*Pisasu!*' he would call them. Devil! Anything could set him off: when he was served food late; when the other tenants complained about his daughters; when his daughters complained about the other tenants; when he had too much toddy and began ranting about his late wife and his life. Sometimes that curse would be accompanied by a raining from his withered belt; during such an explosive episode, Thenmozhi wished for the comfort she used to receive from the folds of her mother's sari as well as her arms.

---

[2] A *lungi* is a sarong or lower garment wrapped around the waist.

The girls learnt very early that the best way to avoid any trouble with their father was to avoid any communication with him.

It was Venkat mama who came up with a solution to his employee's predicament during a visit to check on his welfare. Next to her father's discoloured singlet and old chequered *lungi*, Venkat mama's crisp white long-sleeved shirt, dark pants and black-rimmed spectacles made him look even more successful and respectable. The two men spoke quietly for a while and then revealed to Thenmozhi that a part-time job had been arranged for her.

'Listen!' her father raised a warning finger. 'Venkat mama is being so generous in helping us. Don't embarrass me by misbehaving at work and being lazy, or you will get the belt.'

She could feel the tension in her whole body as her ears pricked for the opening of the front door. Her nimble fingers worked deftly, buffing the metal as fast as she could until her arms ached.

Just as she replaced the last piece back on display, she heard squeals of delight from the children outside. Their father was back! Her throat ran dry and her heart began to pound when she heard the click of the key on the door. Too late!

'Amma not at home?' he asked as he stepped in. She shook her head.

He dumped his work bag onto the sofa and threw his arms up towards the ceiling to give himself a good stretch. 'Come, I need a massage.'

With his chequered lungi, singlet stretched tight over his big belly and black-rimmed spectacles cast aside on the side table, he no longer looked as respectable as he did in public. She had to kneel beside him on the bed in order to knead his calves and thighs. On that day of the very first massage, his hand had just rested innocently against the back of her knee. But over the days, with each subsequent session, he got bolder and she now had to force herself to hold in the helplessness, shame, terror and tears as he touched places she would otherwise never allow. During the very first violation she had tried to push him and run away, but her struggle died after his grip on her tightened and he whispered fiercely that one sentence: 'Do you want me to tell your father that you have been disobedient?'

The servants would have surely seen her tears as she walked out of the gate but as usual, they continued with their respective responsibilities as if nothing was out of the ordinary.

The night air in the room was warm and filled with the musty odour of sweaty bodies, dusty surfaces and stale food. She barely had two mouthfuls of rice and vegetables for dinner that night. Her father, always the first to eat, had been unusually ravenous. She allowed her sisters have their fill from what was left while she darned a tear in her *pavadai*.

As with every other night since the start of those episodes, she lay sleepless on her old, limp mattress for a long while. Her damp, outgrown blouse clung even more uncomfortably to her body. Her mind was thick with the confusion about what possible unforgiveable thing she could have done to bring this unfortunate situation upon herself. She could not shake off that wrenching feeling in her stomach, caused not just by hunger but more by the fear of having to relive the same terror the next day, and the next. There was absolutely nothing she could do about it; nothing, except to utter a silent, fervent prayer that he would not raise any complaint to her father and that her father should recover soon so that she could stop work.

Outside, some drunken men were shouting, '*Merdeka! Merdeka!*'[3] She didn't know nor cared about what those words meant. Her yearning was for their life back in India and for her mother, the only one with whom she could talk, laugh and do just about anything that came spontaneously to a child. Here, despite the crowded streets and cramped accommodation, she was all alone. She uttered another prayer: her father should be able to save enough for all of them to return home, to the place where she could feel the wind on her face, the *padi* brushing against her legs and the wet earth beneath her feet and live freely within the sanctuary of her own community.

1980

From the singing, Manju knew Prakash was behind her, but she couldn't quicken her pace because the after-office crowd on the pavements was at its peak. Prakash caught up with her and began singing again.

'*Netru rathiri, yammaa … thookkam pochchidi, yammaa …*'[4]

'You bloody bastard!' she snapped. She was already uncomfortable from the perspiration caused by the remaining heat of the evening sun. She didn't need Prakash's presence to add to the discomfort.

'Why? Is it a crime to sing?' Prakash asked with feigned innocence.

---

[3] Independence.

[4] Last night, *yammaa* … sleep *pochchidi*, *yammaa*.

'It's about *what* you're singing!'

'What's wrong? I'm just singing about not being able to sleep last night.' She wished fervently for one of the buses to come crashing into the bastard.

The red-and-white public buses were already queuing in front of the bus stop crammed with commuters, all earnestly looking out for their respective bus numbers. Each bus gulped in a bellyful of people before moving off.

Manju could not believe how grossly she had initially misjudged Prakash. After her O-levels, and after months of scouring the newspapers and futile interviews, she was employed as a salesgirl in an electrical department store. She was grateful when this young, respectable-looking co-worker took the initiative to show her the ropes and give her hints on how to hook the customer on a purchase. Within a matter of weeks, though, another side of Prakash emerged, and her gratitude degenerated into disgust.

She blamed it all on the misguided fantasies that Tamil movies portrayed in both the cinema as well as on TV: the hero teases the heroine for fun; the heroine secretly enjoys the teasing; the hero fights bad guys to protect the helpless heroine; the hero and the heroine then fall in love and celebrate with song and dance and live happily ever after. Prakash was a Tamil movie buff and, during slow moments at the store, he and his buddies would openly discuss the latest releases. They would analyse everything: the dance moves, lyrics, melodies, hero's fighting style and heroine's looks, clothes and body.

Once, Prakash and his buddies were discussing the tight-fitting, midriff-revealing blouse worn in a movie by the actress Silk Smitha.

Manju was standing nearby, dusting the shelves.

'Eh, Manju!' Prakash called out to her. 'You look so much like Silk; you should also become an actress. But you must change the way you dress. Too boring. Otherwise, you won't make money.'

Howls of laughter followed. She looked down at her decently tailored *churidar* suit[5] and was engulfed by an overwhelming mix of anger and humiliation that lingered right through her lunch at a nearby coffeeshop. She could not enjoy her noodles and soyabean drink but forced them down her throat. It was a sin to waste food and money.

She had once contemplated lodging a complaint about Prakash's conduct. But after considering that her supervisor kept in his office a big wall poster of a bright yellow bikini-clad model, and that he would occasionally also come over to Prakash's group to join the banter, Manju was convinced that she would hit a brick wall. Her only consolation was sharing her frustrations with her female colleagues, most of whom had been subjected, at some point and in some way, to the taunts of Prakash or other male counterparts. 'What to do? These men are all like that,' one of the salesgirls commented when Manju first talked about it.

Thankfully, her bus arrived soon. She quickly boarded it and pretended not to hear Prakash shout, 'Bye, *kannu*!'[6]

Once she reached home—a neat but austere three-room HDB apartment—her mother Thenmozhi quickly

---

[5] Indian dress comprised of long tight-fitting trousers, worn by both men and women, paired with a tunic-like shirt called a *kameez* or *kurta*.

[6] An endearment denoting familiarity.

made her some hot tea. As Manju sipped her tea and cooled herself under the hall's ceiling fan, she updated her mother about the day's customers and sales. But she would never mention Prakash, because she knew without a doubt that her mother would first interrogate Manju about where she could have gone wrong to attract such unwanted attention. She knew her mother would never talk about such matters to her father because her mother would be the first one to receive a slap, followed by the accusation that she had been lax in bringing up the children properly.

Later that evening, while ironing of her father's and brother's uniform as she usually did, she wished for the thousandth time that she could quit her job. But she didn't want to go through another difficult job-hunting experience, which would definitely be made worse by the oncoming recession. Manju had overheard a neighbour talking about it to her mother. From time to time, the neighbour would stop by on her way back from work. She would pull aside the thin curtain that covered the window overlooking the common corridor and talk about the outside world to her mother, a housewife with no education.

Quitting without another job in hand was also out of the question. Her father's salary as a postman was barely sufficient to meet the educational needs of her sister and brother, who were still in secondary school. They also needed to start planning and saving for Manju's future wedding requirements.

It was just after seven when her sister came home after completing her homework at a classmate's place and was promptly scolded by her mother. Her brother came home close to eight, after enjoying an hour or so of colour TV at his friend's home. He asked for some tea, and her mother quietly obliged. Manju could never understand this double standard of allowing her brother to go over to friends' homes but not her sister or herself.

Her mother appeared in the room to broach the topic of marriage again.

'So, tell me, when?' her mother pressed on.

'I don't know,' Manju replied with a defiant shrug. 'Do we have money?' That never failed to silence her mother and buy time. Her mother sighed and left the room.

As she plowed the heavy iron against the clothes of the males of the house, her heart sank with the uncertainty of her future. Her next stage in life weighed critically on securing the right man and she knew she was on her own in navigating the hurdles to achieve this. She'd be a goner if she was fooled and got stuck with someone like Prakash.

2019

It was past three when Anjali finally felt the hunger pangs and went up to Chill Out, the café located within the premises of her company. She couldn't eat at lunchtime, not just because she had no appetite but more because she did not want to eat with anyone. This was how it had been for the past two weeks—lack of appetite, difficulty with sleep, no mood for socialising, lost satisfaction at work. No amount of retail therapy had helped. In the past week, she had splurged on a pair of running shoes, trackpants, a handbag, a jacket and a pullover. They had brought her no joy.

The popular steak with mushroom sauce, which came with a complimentary cappuccino, was still available. After placing her order, she took out the letter that had arrived from Ma, who was still in Mallipandi. She was reading it a day late due to the dawn-to-dusk workdays she was putting in on an analytics solution for a hypermart.

The last time Anjali had gone to Mallipandi was two years ago, with her parents, older brother Ajit and her grandmother, Thenmozhi Aachi. After her husband's funeral, Aachi had at first suggested, later insisted then finally demanded that she return to her motherland to live out the rest of her life there. Mallipandi had not changed, not by the stories Aachi had told Anjali when she was a child. There was no proper public transport, no malls, no Internet, no Wi-Fi. Just miles of *padi*, clusters of chickens, herds of goats and hordes of relatives and friends who were excited about these rare visitors from Singapore. From those stories of Mallipandi, Anjali knew that, despite living most of her life in Singapore, Aachi's heart was still rooted in India.

Five months after settling down in Mallipandi, Aachi died peacefully in her sleep. Anjali's parents were there now, commemorating her first death anniversary. Deadlines and targets had prevented Anjali from accompanying them. Ajit had already left for Canada, where he had cinched an opportunity to work as an engineer.

Anjali had only half-read the letter when her mobile pinged with an incoming text. It was Santosh, the team lead, wanting to meet in an hour to discuss another tender, and insisting on the meeting even though the rest of the team had already left the office.

That riddled her with discomfort. She did not want to be alone with him. She pushed away her steak, which was not even half-eaten. She had lost her appetite again.

Santosh was intelligent. The #MeToo movement had taught him to be more covert with his own moves. She once overheard him during lunch, as he sat at an adjacent table and discussed it with another male colleague. 'Can't believe how stupid these fellas are, leaving around evidence.' Santosh left no incriminating e-mail, WhatsApp messages or Instagram posts. Anjali would not be able to prove anything in case something did happen. In fact, Santosh could turn the tables and accuse Anjali as the initiator.

There were witnesses. Santosh and Anjali were at Chill Out, amidst its usual dinner and drinks crowd. They were discussing the hypermart project when he mentioned that he would be recommending her for a promotion in her staff appraisal report. Maybe it was the combination of the bourbon and the elation of being affirmed by a capable senior that made her lean forward to squeeze his knee to show her appreciation. He just smiled and didn't seem to make anything of it.

Or so she thought.

One week later, during a party at a holiday chalet rented by a coworker, Santosh asked her to accompany him to his car to help bring out more drinks. It was parked quite a distance away, close to a deserted beach area. She was totally unprepared for him pushing her against the bonnet, groping her and insisting that she kiss him before he let her go. When she finally managed to push him away in disgust, he laughed and then said casually, 'You know, I can make things go smoothly for you or you can have it the hard way. You decide.'

He collected his bagful of six-packs from the boot and walked away.

She mustered up the courage to talk about it only a few days later. She was not particularly close to anyone at work. Everybody was too busy to form any bond deeper than what was superficially cordial. She decided to bring it up during a project discussion with Carrie, one of her more senior teammates.

'I'm sure he meant no harm, darling. It was a party, after all,' Carrie replied in her fake American accent. 'It's okay, just relax. You don't need to act like a frightened little virgin.'

That remark had stunned Anjali. It left her in a limbo. Should she rely on the opinion of a long-serving employee or continue to believe what her long-held values were telling her?

She looked at the text again and wondered what Santosh was up to now. She was already experiencing the disadvantages of rejecting him that night at the chalet: the avalanche of tasks assigned her, undue criticism on her work and, contrary to what Santosh and promised, a mediocre staff appraisal report.

Thinking back, she realised she had made a stupid move by informing Carrie about the incident. She had totally overlooked the occasional muted flirting between Carrie and Santosh, which would take place in the pantry, café or lift. Carrie would definitely have told Santosh. In fact, that appraisal report came just after Anjali's complaint to Carrie.

She texted Santosh back. 'Not feeling well. Going home.' Then she switched off her handphone and headed home.

Inside the quiet, half-empty carpark, just before getting into the car, she made a conscious attempt to read the remaining lines of the letter—her parents were flying back to Singapore over the coming weekend.

Her thoughts drifted to Mallipandi and Aachi as she drove through the smooth, pre-peak-hour expressway. Aachi must have led a difficult life, being poor and laden with family responsibilities from a young age. But life those days would probably have not been so complicated as in these modern times. Aachi had said she'd never been to school nor to work, so her whole life had been about family.

Ma's life was so different. She completed her O-levels, continued to work even after marriage and scrimped on household expenses so that Ajit and Anjali could be educated all the way up to their Masters. Like Aachi, Ma had also told Anjali many stories about her own life, including her experience with an asshole called Prakash. Ma had always frowned on coarse language so Anjali couldn't help laughing to herself at the thought of her mother calling him a 'bloody bastard'.

At the last traffic light stop just before reaching her condominium, she switched on her handphone and located the last message Ma had sent before leaving for Mallipandi. That had been a week before National Day. The link came with the message: *This was sixty years ago.* It led to a video clip where the elation of the people could be heard after the 1959 elections.

'*Merdeka!*' cheered Singapore's founding father, and a huge roar rose from the crowd.

'*Lagi sekali yang bersemangat*,'[7] he stirred them. '*MERDEKA!*' Another roar burst forth.

Home. The lush, thick curtains over tightly shut windows blocked out the irritating sounds of the traffic building up outside and highlighted the soft whir of the air-conditioning. The coolness brought tranquility and a certain clarity to life. She stood in the middle of the spacious yet cosy living room and took a deep breath. With the full force of her voice, she raised up her arms and screamed out, 'You bloody bastard!'

There, she was finally able to say what both respect and fear had prevented her from saying these past few weeks. Funny what a story and a video clip could do.

Anjali could not wait for the weekend, to tell Ma all that had happened while she was away in Mallipandi.

A sense of freedom engulfed her and with it came a fresh wave of hunger. She picked up her handphone and ordered pizza with hot lemon tea.

---

[7] Once again with passion.

49

5

Papaji's Desire

Surinder Kaur

Having completed her studies in Toronto, Daljit returned to Singapore to a unique homecoming. Papaji was elated but Bibi wore a disgruntled look. She had sent off a decent, reserved daughter with long hair but received a shorthaired, outspoken, western-educated child from overseas. Not a fair exchange, she reckoned.

She blurted out in frustration. 'Your short hair looks terrible! Why did you cut it? Now nobody will marry you.' Such blunt words from Bibi sent a shiver down Daljit's spine. Papaji just kept silent during her outburst. Despite this, he was beaming with pride. She had graduated and that was all that mattered to him.

Daljit recalled her childhood days when Papaji allowed her to have short hair while her sisters were compelled to keep their hair long. They always had a hard time with Bibi on hair-washing days as she would scrub the daylights out of their scalps using excessive shampoo. Eventually, her sisters would troop out of the toilet with their eyes reddened in their zombie-like faces.

Papaji always regarded her as his son. He even coaxed Daljit into participating in hockey to release all that pent-up energy and restlessness during her teens. That became a passion for Daljit, and she could not live without hockey. Hockey practices, matches and extra fitness exercises took over her life. Definitely, he knew she was different. And she was the only one who detested shopping for clothes, shoes and make-up, considering them a great waste of time.

Papaji's two elder daughters had already settled on partners whom they courted, defying his warnings. 'You still want to date that *ang moh*,[1] you leave this house, Guddi,' Papaji shouted.

'But Papaji, we are in love.'

'Yes, love and love now but later, he leaves you. Who will want you then? We are a small Punjabi community, and everyone will eventually know.'

After numerous squabbles, Papaji gave in. He had to accept their partners who were not Punjabi. This got tongues wagging as Papaji was an established businessman and a known figure in the community. Papaji kept all his dejection to himself. But one day, he asked Daljit a question that shocked her. 'Tell me how you would feel if I introduced a Punjabi boy to you.'

'Papaji, you mean … marriage? But I landed just like two weeks ago!' Daljit protested.

'I know, but you are my last hope for getting a Punjabi son-in-law. Your sisters have made their choices. Just give it a try and see if he is suitable, for my sake.'

'Okay, Papaji.' Daljit reluctantly agreed to do it out of respect for him. Arranged marriages did work despite many negative comments about them. Punjabi parents persisted in arranging partners for their children wherever they were in the world. It was a combination of

---

[1] A racial descriptor used to refer to white people that is sometimes seen as a pejorative epithet, it is mainly used in Singapore and Taiwan, and to a lesser extent Malaysia and Thailand.

love and fear that made them persist in finding the best partner particularly for their daughters, lest they were left on the shelf.

The day of the meeting arrived but Daljit was not forewarned about the potential groom's arrival. Meanwhile, she was in a pair of shorts and worn-out t-shirt so she hastily changed into her jeans and a decent blouse after much nagging from Bibi.

'*Sat Sri Akal*,' Papaji and the turbaned man both greeted each other with clasped hands.

'So, where is your son?' Papaji asked.

'He is coming in a while.'

'Daljit! Daljit, come downstairs.'

'Yes, Papaji.'

It was an unexpected and unwelcome moment for Daljit. She was doing this for her Papaji. His happiness mattered to her. But what if it all backfired? She dragged herself down the stairs and reached the office table where Papaji sat most nights to have his Scotch whisky after an exhausting day of work in his tailor shop. She braced herself.

'This is my daughter Daljit.' Immediately, the boy's father raised his brows at her short, boyish hairstyle. The look of disapproval was evident on his face.

'Daughter, when did you come back from Canada and what did you study there?'

'Just a fortnight ago. I did English literature and history.'

'Good. My son is doing medicine. And he is in his final year at the local university.'

Then the boy's father stared intently at Daljit for a moment before he spoke again, 'You know that when you marry my son, you must grow your hair long. You will also have to help out in the kitchen.'

Daljit smiled but was uneasy with his bluntness. He was already planning what she had to do. It was absurd.

Long hair was mandated by the Sikh religion for both males and females, but Papaji had cut his hair. Daljit thought she could get away with this since Papaji had set a bad example. But she could dream on. Males got away with it owing to the double standards in the community. She had cut her hair in Toronto during her studies as it was a chore to wash her long, thick hair. Also, she only sparingly used the coconut oil at university that Bibi had packed for her, although Bibi had told her it was good for her scalp and would help her think better.

Papaji replied, 'I think my daughter will be busy working. After all, she has a degree.'

Daljit was proud that Papaji stated his opinion succinctly.

'Yes, surely working is a good thing,' remarked the suitor's father condescendingly. Suddenly, another turbaned man appeared and greeted Papaji with a grumpy expression. He had a thick beard which covered most of his face. It was the doctor whom Papaji intended for her. She was in a blouse and faded jeans with short hair and the suitor, his long hair in a turban, was dressed conventionally. What an awkward pair!

Following the turbaned suitor were his sisters and mother. Daljit was not even properly attired to allure the groom, much less given any prior warning that the entire family was turning up to view her like some pedigree cat. She had to greet his two sisters and mother who looked awfully snooty. They were dressed in traditional Punjabi *salwar* suits.[2] Daljit was excluded from their intimate conversation as they muttered softly to each other, indifferent to her presence.

Then the boy's mother abruptly asked, 'What did you study?' Daljit told her.

'Oh, literature. So, you will become a teacher.'

'Yes, most probably.'

'You cannot be dressed like this nor have such short hair if you marry my son.'

'Yes, your husband mentioned this.'

'We are a proper Punjabi family, and we follow the Sikh religion strictly. You will have to fit in.'

Daljit was stunned as she registered the woman's stress on the words 'fit in'. This left Daljit with little room to be her own woman. Now it was getting scary and Daljit shifted in her seat uneasily.

'My daughters are both professionals. One is working as an accountant and the other is a lawyer.'

'You must be very proud of them,' Daljit interjected sarcastically.

His haughty sisters and mother did not seem interested in this arranged meeting and decided to walk around the neighbourhood, much to Daljit's relief. She thought that this family was too hoity-toity for her. She shrank at the thought of living with such a family. Her family was laidback and seldom went to the temple after the girls became teenagers.

The turbaned suitor stated to his father, 'Please do not drink too much.' Papaji had handed the old

---

[2] The *salwar* suit is an Indian outfit comprised of a pair of trousers (*salwar*) and a tunic (*kameez*) that is usually paired with a long scarf (*dupatta*).

man a glass of whiskey, but the boy gave his father a disapproving look.

'This is Kalwant.' The suitor gave her a half-smile. She nodded.

'You should not drink,' he repeated to his father. This irritated Daljit. Why couldn't he loosen up?

'Well, son, this is a joyous occasion for both families. A small peg of whisky does no harm.'

The suitor took off after the sisters and mother. The father continued his conversation with Daljit. He seemed more accommodating than his son. Daljit was sitting with her Papaji after the boy's family eventually left. Papaji was quietly holding his glass of Scotch but seem contented that Daljit had allowed him to introduce her to a Punjabi boy. Daljit spoke up as she felt pressured. 'Papaji, the boy is so traditional. How will I fit into this family?'

'Let us just wait for their reply. Don't jump the gun.'

'But the boy didn't seem at all interested. And I feel like I'm marrying the entire family rather than him. We hardly talked to each other.'

'I just wanted you to meet him first. That's all.' Papaji continued sipping his Scotch.

Daljit was exasperated by the whole thing and walked off. Hopefully, this foolish saga would be forgotten soon. It seemed like an eternity. Two weeks had passed but no updates from Papaji. Daljit thought that the family was surely taking their time to decide.

In the meantime, Bibi was rebuking her for keeping her hair short and warning her to grow it back. Frustrated, Daljit stormed out of the room to avoid her mother's constant nagging.

Daljit was curious about the suitor's answer to the proposal. She summoned up enough courage to ask Papaji. 'What happened to the suitor, Papaji?'

'The boy's family asked for a big dowry as his son is going to become a doctor. He said it would help defray the expenses for his medical studies. I told them that I am not doing that.'

'Papaji, I am sorry.'

'Sorry about what? You are not going to their home to cook and slave for them. You are educated and will work. They need to know your worth. Forget about them.'

'Papaji, it would be easier if I were a boy.'

'Don't be silly. How would being a boy make it easier?'

'No need to give a dowry. And no need to submit to silly demands of long hair and making chapattis for the whole family.'

Papaji smiled and went off to do some work in his shop. Daljit could not complete the conversation to find out his true feelings. She felt that she had disappointed him by being a girl. She had been feeling like this for a long time. She would be his son by not marrying and taking care of Papaji for the rest of her life. Yes, that was the only way to repay him for giving her a university education overseas.

The years went by and Daljit settled into her job as an editor at a publishing company. One by one, her sisters got married and Daljit was left, as Bibi would put it, on the shelf. Papaji was concerned about his youngest daughter.

'Daljit, find a partner like your sisters and get married.'

'Papaji, I do not want to make the four mistakes you made. Marrying Bibi and having three girls.'

'You remembered exactly the absurd words I uttered while having my tipple,' he smiled. 'You know I never meant it. Find a partner.'

'But it's too late, Papaji. I am already thirty-seven. How am I going to find a partner? Most of the men I know are married or not Punjabi.'

Papaji listened and felt helpless in this situation. He wanted his daughter to be contented like his friend's married daughter. But Daljit was different. She was not a typical Punjabi girl but had lived in Toronto on her own for several years, which had made her independent and resilient. Daljit saw the look of despair on her Papaji's face and offered words of consolation.

'Papaji, I do not need anyone. I have you and Bibi. That is more than enough.'

Bibi, who overheard this, was outraged by Daljit's emotional expression.

'You think this will solve our problem—you staying single? Who will look after you after we die?'

What an absurd assertion! Now Daljit lost it and shouted at her. 'Bibi, why can't you accept that I am different from your other daughters?'

'You must marry for your own good!' Bibi continued to lambast her.

'Now, it doesn't mean marriage will bring ultimate happiness. Look at Cousin Jaspal who has a part-time husband.' Daljit was still speaking in a high-pitched angry tone.

'What do you mean, part-time?' Now Bibi was listening instead of being on the offensive.

'He has a Filipino girlfriend on the side and does not come home sometimes. It is not as easy as you think.

Jaspal has two young kids and cannot walk out of the marriage as she is financially dependent on her husband. She is looking for a job now.'

'I know it will be not be easy, but a suitable partner will bring some joy to your life, Daljit. And children are the greatest joy in a woman's life. Do you understand?'

'*Aiyah*,[3] Bibi, I do not want to think about all these things. I am past my prime. Who will want me now?'

Papaji interrupted this intense exchange by straightening out Bibi's views. 'That is why we educated our daughters so they can be independent and also financially independent. It is no longer necessary to worry about marriage.'

Daljit was impressed by Papaji. This should shut Bibi up.

Bibi gave him a defeated look and went into the kitchen to prepare lunch. However, Bibi heard remarks from other women such as, 'Your daughter okay or not? She is still not married till now.'

Or her Chinese neighbour once remarked out of concern, 'Tell your daughter not to be too fussy. Just marry a simple boy *lah*.'

On days such as these, Daljit could smell the medicated oil on Bibi's forehead, and Bibi would mourn loudly so that Papaji could hear her after she returned from the neighbourhood wet market.

'You don't have to put up with remarks about your daughter being unmarried, but I have to when the ladies in the neighbourhood make remarks.'

---

[3] Exclamation to express disappointment.

Papaji would ignore her and carry on with the sewing in his shop, only stopping to sternly tell her to her to go upstairs to mourn about such trivial matters.

This went on for a while until her sisters had children to occupy her, and Bibi gradually gave up on Daljit.

One day, Bibi approached her and said, 'Take this box.'

'What is in the box, Bibi?' Daljit asked softly.

'All the jewellery I bought over the years to prepare for your wedding day. It is all in this box. You can have it and do whatever you like with it since you are going to remain unmarried.'

Daljit opened it and found intricately designed gold bangles, earrings and a chain glistening in the light that shone through the window.

Daljit was hurt by her words and replied, 'Bibi, you can keep them. I obviously do not need them as I am earning enough to support myself.'

Papaji observed from afar that a storm was brewing and stepped in.

'Listen, Daljit, your Bibi is just concerned though she acts tough like she cannot be bothered anymore.'

'How can I convince her that I am fine being single?' answered Daljit

'You cannot because she is as stubborn as you are. She is a traditional woman from Punjab who believes that marriage completes a woman. You are born in Singapore with a more liberal view about things and times have changed, but Bibi holds on to tradition as it gives her stability and security.'

Just then, Bibi started crying and hitting her chest in a dramatic way. 'This girl will kill me by her stinging remarks. She does not know her mother's heart.'

Daljit reflected on this drama and decided to placate her Bibi by saying that she would still try to marry, but Bibi knew that her daughter was just saying what she wanted to hear. She was resigned to the fact that one of her daughters would remain a spinster and her community would make her feel like a failure as she could not get all of them married off.

Papaji watched both the women and tried to pacify them as much as he could. He still wanted a Punjabi son-in-law but accepted the fact that this was the way his daughter wanted to lead her life. As long as she was happy, he was too.

6

Home Without Walls

Phyllis Wong

Mei Chan locks the wrought iron gate behind her with a soft clink. Next, she unlocks the wooden door, pushes with both hands and gently closes the door behind her, careful not to let her neighbours notice her return. She calls out, 'I'm home!' She has started doing this recently although only silence greets her. The sound of her voice evokes memories of Pa reading the newspaper with the radio on, Ma shouting from the kitchen asking her if she had eaten. These memories comfort her. Pa passed away from lung disease when Mei Chan was only seventeen. Ma passed away after a two-year battle with liver cancer. Then, Mei Chan was thirty. After Ma's death, she buried herself in work. Not that she didn't miss them. There was no time to grieve, until now. Like a train nearing a station, the pace of life is slowing. Mei Chan retired a month ago. She had planned to travel, to do all the things she couldn't during her fifty years of work since she entered the workforce. But COVID-19 tossed her plans aside.

Mei Chan puts her bag down and settles onto the sofa. Stretching her legs out, she stares vacantly at the television in front of her, not understanding a word of Korean. These days, she spends hours watching Korean drama until she falls asleep. Time is plenty with little to do. Stuck at home with no office to go, no family and friends to meet up with. Socially distanced for the greater good during virus time. Normally she reads the English subtitles. Today, she feels so drained that watching takes up too much energy. She doesn't feel like going out with the pandemic numbers being all that the news is about. But thoughts pour relentlessly into her head, like crickets in the night.

Mei Chan feels the chill from the standing fan oscillating next to the television. She drapes a shawl lengthwise from her feet to her neck. Her mind drifts back to the time she donned suits and her secretary appeared at the press of a button. Now she has no deadlines to meet. No appointments to keep other than to doctors. The only stress she faces is when the fridge is empty, like Old Mother Hubbard's. Then, she has no choice but to put on her floppy hat, unfold her blue-and-white polka-dotted umbrella and pop sunshades over her thick glasses. She wears a double layer of transition spectacles with sunglasses as any glare her left eye catches, imprints a light image in that eye. This bright oval-shaped glow stays for a few minutes before fading, returning and leaving as suddenly to restore normal vision. Well, normal enough with floaters flitting like flies in both eyes. Dragging the red canvas trolley with reluctant wheels and a metal frame that refuses to stand firm when full, she staggers to the wet market two bus stops away. Trudging from stall to stall gives her no pleasure. She detests getting her ankles dirty with water flicking onto her feet from the ground. She feels the damp despite wearing long pants and socks. And she is afraid of touching raw meat. So, she eats small portions and tries to replenish her pantry every six weeks. Mei Chan could shop at supermarkets, but the range of food is limited and more expensive compared to the wet markets. She has the means to dine at restaurants, but the idea of eating out alone no longer appeals to her. Food sustains life. Without company to share it with, food is like pizza without the toppings.

Mei Chan didn't use this name of hers in the years she sat behind a large desk. She was vice president, finance of a public-listed publishing house. She was known as Faye Wong, the same name as the Cantopop singer. Mei Chan was Faye Wong before the younger Faye came to fame. Mei Chan can croon like a professional. Her voice helped raise funds at charity balls. Her performance gowns are still hanging in her wardrobes. Glittering, figure-hugging gowns that clung beautifully to her petite frame. Just as she retired from the job that paid her well and locked away her fancy gowns, Mei Chan put away Faye Wong. She is back to the name given by Pa: translated from the Cantonese, it means 'really beautiful'. She remembers Ma telling her, '*Wah!* You dress like a bird. You are actually quite pretty. It's a pity you are short of a few inches.'

Now she lives alone. As the television continues to change scenes, Mei Chan's thoughts wander through the streets of time. Then, home was a shared space.

Home with Ma and Pa was a house bustling with family. Ma ruled the nest. Pa was quiet and often not at home. Mei Chan is the youngest of four girls and a boy. The family of seven lived in a corner unit of a row of single-storeyed shophouses.

Mei Chan recalls Ma's beef noodle stall on the street in front of their house. The main door was kept open to facilitate the retrieval of more *mee*[1] or *kway teow*[2] or beef cubes and slices from the fridge in the living room. And to get pails of water from the kitchen to wash the dishes. Pa was a courier for Chinese migrants. He helped his friends deliver goods like sewing machines, clothes, medicine and money to their families in Guangdong. They trusted him and paid him for services. Although the post was slow, grateful relatives would write to acknowledge receipt and thank them. Each trip on a steamer ship took Pa away for at least three months.

Ma, Pa and their friends were young people who had left their homeland to eke a living. The men worked outdoors as labourers and street hawkers. The women worked as domestic helpers. Known as *Ah Ma Chey*, they wore white tops and black satin trousers with their hair braided in a single strand that descended to their waists. The folks spent frugally so as to send back their earnings to support their kin in China. Some had wives and children in China. Some married after moving to Singapore, like Ma and Pa. They met in the island-state, married, had children and settled in the country that beckoned them with the promise of shelter from poverty and a new life of home away from home.

Pa could read and write in Cantonese. He was born into a landowning family that became impoverished when the Japanese occupied China. Pa and Ma likely met at the clan association where all the villagers gathered for mutual support. They shared stories of braving months at sea and sleeping in the hot lower decks of

[1] Noodles.
[2] A popular noodle dish with flat rice noodles.

cargo steamships. They shared the goal of hard work to provide the basic needs for themselves and the loved ones they had left behind.

Mei Chan remembers that Ma and Pa's friends used to visit their home and Pa helped them write letters as they dictated. He didn't charge them. Sometimes they gave him a few dollars for coffee or brought fruit for Ma. They spoke to Ma and Pa in their Guangdong village patois that was totally unlike Cantonese. Over time, Mei Chan and her siblings picked up a smattering of phrases. Mei Chan recalls being asked the question by the aunties in their quaint sing-song manner, *'Nei hai kai sui ge nui zay?'* (Whose daughter are you?)

Mei Chan's parents talked with their children in a plain brand of Cantonese. Even when the older kids started attending school, only Cantonese was used at home. The children spoke in Cantonese among themselves unless they had secrets that they didn't want Ma to catch a whiff of.

Mei Chan remembers her family eating at the round marble table in the living room, directly in view of the noodle stall. Other than on the first two days of Chinese New Year when the stall was closed, customers were not turned away.

Mei Chan's position as the youngest and smallest in size exempted her from most duties until she grew older. Her three elder sisters shared the load of housework and noodle-stall work with Ma. Mei Chan sat in a corner of the living room, her nose buried in a book. Or she did her schoolwork when Ma's cane landed on her. Mei Chan grimaces with the memory. Thankfully Ma's voice usually reached her before the whack, so she had a moment to scurry off her seat to safety. Mei Chan loved reading. From the minute she returned from school, she would sit on the green chair in the corner until Ma scolded her or nature called. Sometimes Ma would remind her to eat, 'Come to help lay the table.' Only then would she uncurl herself from the chair to set the table for Ma, Pa, Ka Chey (eldest sister), Ko Ko (elder brother), Yi Chey (second sister) and Sum Chey (third sister). Often nobody remembered to tell her that dinner was ready because they were too busy and didn't notice her huddled over her book. By the time her stomach rumbled and she reluctantly emerged from the pages, she would often find the table cleared of food. Ma would tell her, 'Everyone has eaten, and all the leftovers have already been kept in the fridge.' Ma refused to cook noodles for her. Ka Chey kindly did.

Meals were a feast on special occasions like Chinese New Year, Pa's birthday and on the days when Ma prayed to the deities of her Chinese folk religion before her conversion to Christianity. Only at such meals did the family consume a whole chicken, big prawns, abalone and Ma's special steamed whole melon soup. Pa and Ko Ko each took a drumstick. Ka Chey liked the breast meat. The other two ate whatever was left to choose from. Mei Chan was jealous. While Ma divided fruit like longans, lychees and grapes into little piles for each child, there were only two drumsticks on a whole chicken, rare treats for the two men of the house.

Everyone was assigned duties except Ko Ko and Pa. Ma and Ka Chey took turns to man the stall or cook meals for the family. Yi Chey washed the clothes. Sum Chey did the general cleaning, mopping the floor and furniture till she escaped to live in a hostel while she pursued a course in nursing. When Mei Chan grew older, her added task was to boil drinking water and buy coffee every morning or afternoon, depending on which session of school she attended. The older girls rotated to wash dishes, except Mei Chan. At this recollection, Mei Chan laughs as she remembers Ma telling her, 'You break everything!' Ko Ko was Ma's favourite. He had no duties except to study. He could go out with his friends any time he wanted. Mei Chan was grounded. Ma used to say, '*Chap yik li chao fei chor hui.*' (Give you wings, you will fly away.) Mei Chan asked for Ma to send her to piano and art lessons. Ma said that would take too many bowls of noodles to pay. But Ko Ko got the encyclopedia set and hi-fi set he asked for.

Despite the privileges accorded to the youngest child that she received, Mei Chan's resentment grew as she grew. As she lies on the sofa, she recalls waking up early one morning in the room she shared with Pa and Ma. The room was still dark when she crept to the dressing table and took the green hair gel Pa used to slick his hair down with. Ma was snoring. Pa had left for one of his trips. 'Boys are more loved than girls. I want to be a boy,' Mei Chan declared as she dug her little fingers into the plastic container, swiping and wiping the contents onto her short hair. She parted her hair at one side with Pa's fine-toothed comb. Pushing her hair behind her ears, she muttered in satisfaction, 'Now I look like a boy.'

She remembers this scene clearly because the next second she was terrified. Ma, who was lying on the bed with her face to wall, turned to her other side. 'Whew!

Glad she didn't wake up,' Mei Chan breathed. She left the room quickly, making as little noise as possible before Ma. Everyone was still asleep. With the bathroom door locked and turning the tap to a trickle to minimise the sound, Mei Chan frantically washed her hair to remove any trace of the gel. It took many rounds of water and shampoo to rid of the sticky Tancho hair pomade on the matted mess.[3] When Ma awoke, she asked, 'Why did you wash your hair so early?' Mei Chan mumbled an excuse and escaped without Ma discovering the secret of her transient transformation.

One day Mei Chan could not hold back, *'Ma, lei pin sum'* (Ma, you are unfair). Ma was squatting next to the noodle stall, washing dishes. When Ma heard Mei Chan, she held out her right palm. She said, *'Sau pan hai yoke'* (The palm is made of flesh). Then she turned her hand over, *'Sau min yao hai yoke'* (The back of the hand is made of flesh). *'Guok pien pin do yao huk'* (Cut either side, my hand bleeds). From that time onwards, Mei Chan stopped saying that Ko Ko was Ma's favourite. Ma's tears were balm to her hurt.

One evening, Ma lifted both her hands in front of Mei Chan. She fanned out her fingers. 'Look,' she said, her voice a blend of firmness and tenderness. 'These ten fingers are of varying lengths. None alike. Each one uniquely made.' Ma continued, 'Short of any of them, I cannot be well and whole. How can I love one more than another? My children are like my fingers.' These stories that Ma and Mei Chan shared remained their secret.

---

[3] Tancho is a sticky, greasy and green hair pomade for men that was very popular in the 1960s and is still available today.

Ma was bedridden in her final months. Mei Chan remembers sitting on the floor next to Ma's bed. Her skin had turned yellow and the stoma bag was hanging on the bedframe. Ma said, 'Mei Chan, if you had not studied so much, you would have married.' Mei Chan told Ma that perhaps she would not have been happy if she had. Ma countered, 'Who is going to look after you when you are old?'

This evening, the assurance that Mei Chan gave Ma to allay her worries echoes as she ponders on the sofa. The movements of the Korean drama keep pace companionably with her interior stories. 'Ma, you don't need to be afraid for me. Jesus will look after me.' Ma closes her eyes. She appears pacified as she clasps her hands over her chest as if in prayer.

As Mei Chan ruminates on her growing years, she realises that her perception that boys were better treated and that girls had to fight for independence and fairness, had shaped her. Mei Chan watched her three sisters get married and move out. Ko Ko got married and stayed in Ma's house. Mei Chan had dated, but no one she liked enough to marry. Ma might have been right: if she had not studied so much, she might not have been 'picky' as Ma said she was. Mei Chan had a secret fear: that of life under one roof with a married sibling after Ma passed on.

Her growing years inculcated in her a spirit to live fully and freely. She single-mindedly strove for financial independence. Her faith thrived on a firm foundation of God-dependence. When she told Ma, 'Jesus will look after me,' she meant it. Her perception that sons were favoured energised her to pour herself into her books. She and Ko Ko were the only two siblings with tertiary education. Mei Chan worked full time on completing pre-university, concurrently pursuing a long-distance professional degree in accountancy from the UK. 'Girls can do as well as boys' was her motto. She entered the workforce at eighteen as an audit clerk. Here was a girl who had been on outings without her family only twice—once with her schoolfriends in Primary Six and once in Secondary One, and a couple of times during the two pre-university years. Those trips were permitted only during school holidays. Ma was protective of her youngest.

Mei Chan spent forty years in the finance sector. She 'retired' with a post-graduate degree that equipped her for social work. Cancer took Ma and two of her sisters away. The 'Big C' caught Mei Chan twenty years ago. But Mei Chan survived. Her perceived crucible of home with Ma playing favourites, and the working world's male bias sharpened her survival instincts. Mei Chan believed Jesus's promise to be her friend from when she was seven.

The hands on the Wedgwood hand-painted clock are pointing to 7 pm. Mei Chan gets up from the sofa. Her sixty-eighth birthday is in three months. She picks up her mobile and texts Ko Ko and Sum Chey. 'Come celebrate the gifts of life with me. Come with your family.' Other than special occasions, they seldom meet. The absence of social connections has never more keenly been felt than during COVID-19. Mei Chan has been living in isolation, going out only for food and medical needs. The gift of the space is purifying. She has discovered the layers of her formation, and found one necessary thing: love, to build relationships and break walls. Now that phase 3 is being progressively calibrated with falling community infections, Mei Chan is hopeful that, by December, she can have her party.

Mei Chan's musings have eaten up time. There is no food in the fridge as usual. She unlocks the door and the gate. This time, she does not try to be unobtrusive so as to avoid her neighbours from hearing her movements. A light reenters her. Her feet seem to float as she crosses the street to the coffeeshop she frequents. 'Hello! Why so late? Come sit at your usual table,' Grace, the server, smiles her welcome.

'Ah! I'm home for dinner,' Mei Chan sighs with pleasure as she sits in a corner furthest from the smells of the stoves.

What is home, she wonders. Not a building behind walls. No, home is as big as a heart open to welcome, without judgement, without expecting others to be like one. A space without walls. Though the family living in it may not agree, they can stay together, united in their care for each other. That night, Mei Chan discovers that 'Home is in the me I am.' She finally comes home to herself.

II

Comfort and Sustenance

7

The Gardeners of Lim Tai See

Aparna Das Sadhukhan

She awoke to a cacophony of mynahs—a sound she had missed the last few days owing to torrential rains every morning. She wondered if a koel would ever choose to make her garden its home. She'd prefer that to the noise but over the last year she had warmed up to the mynahs creating a ruckus on her lawn. Salil disliked those birds and often compared them to the crows back home. They upset him routinely. 'Bloody pests,' he'd often yell while trying to shoo them away with a rolled-up copy of *The Straits Times*. It was a familiar scene most mornings, unless he was travelling.

His disdain was a matter of amusement as much as shock, for he had once told Jhumpa that the Large Billed Crow was part of *Corvus Macrorhyncos*, a native species to Singapore and an aggressive lot, the reason why the government had been culling its flocks in some areas. Jhumpa worried that Salil would write to the NEA[1] and get the mynahs culled too—the government took citizen pleas rather seriously, she had heard.

On days that Salil was travelling, Jhumpa would wake up later than usual. But of late she had discovered the birds of Lim Tai See. Her early morning walks had rewarded her with many a sighting of exotic birds, names

---

[1] National Environment Agency, Singapore.

of which she was incrementally learning, sometimes from the Internet and at times from Auntie Chia, the old lady who lived at the end of Lim Tai See Walk.

Her spirits lifted when Auntie Chia came to her mind. She hurried down the stairs to brew her morning pot of chai, or *cha*, as people from her hometown called it. There was something elegant about how Jhumpa brewed her Darjeeling tea, a manner which perhaps came instinctively only to folks who grew up in and around tea estates. While the tea leaves steeped, she stuck her face inside the airtight tea box and took a deep breath in, the aroma of Orange Pekoe filling her up, conjuring sights and sounds from Jalpaiguri. Brewing tea was one of the few habits she had clung to after moving away from home. Her mother would call it a ritual; Jhumpa, on the other hand, didn't fuss over her tea like her mother but partook of it nevertheless to keep up with the habit. In her few months of living away, she had discovered old habits were the only way she could keep home alive inside her.

Sighing, she closed the lid and made a mental note to ask Auntie Chia where she could find tin boxes like the ones her mother used to store tea.

Jhumpa washed her cup and wondered what to do next. She skipped breakfast on days Salil wasn't home. She was already bored and deliberated if going out for a walk would do her any good in that muggy weather. But she craved company and knew a chat with Auntie Chia would lift her spirits.

As expected, Auntie Chia was tending to her roadside kitchen garden. Her own garden didn't have space left for her to plant any more papaya trees, so she had knocked at all the residents' doors of Lim Tai See Walk, asking their permission to use the patch of land outside every home to create little gardens. She didn't lay claim to any fruit and had told them everyone could enjoy the fruits of her labour as long as they watered the plants.

As Jhumpa strolled past motley vegetable patches, admiring a beautiful blue-pea creeper that Auntie Chia had cleverly planted by a compound wall, she spotted her on her haunches, planting yet another papaya sapling. Before she could exchange greetings with her, Auntie Chia caught sight of her and began talking. At seventy-five, she was still a strong woman with a sharp mind. She loved chatting with passersby and often gifted unsuspecting souls random fruit and vegetables from her garden. She lived alone at the corner of Lim Tai See with her Shih Tzu named Gongzhu, which means 'princess' in Chinese.

'Joopa! How are you? Have you visited the Hoon San Temple or not *aan*? Did you know that it was built in 1920? It is just down Alamanda Grove! You must go what?'

Jhumpa nodded and stifled a giggle at Auntie's pronunciation of her name.

Most people couldn't pronounce it properly in Singapore, but it didn't bother her too much. She was still getting used to the kind of English people spoke here and increasingly found herself conversing with wet-market vendors with confidence by adding a *lah* at the end of every sentence—all Auntie Chia's contribution in making Jhumpa Singapore-ready.

Jhumpa, however, craved conversation in Bengali but learnt that no Bengalis lived in Lim Tai See. Salil barely spoke Bangla, and his English also had a local twang at times. She felt he used it on purpose to make her feel alien. Jhumpa hadn't quite wrapped her head around her marriage. It had all happened in such a hurry that Jhumpa often wondered, while she had a moment to herself in those two weeks before her wedding, if Salil was indeed what she believed him to be.

Salil was a friendly, modern guy who ticked most boxes that Jhumpa cared about. He seemed like a decent chap who shared a common interest in finance, food and tea with Jhumpa. But his rather unassuming personality was what assured Jhumpa.

Jhumpa's aunt in Kolkata was instrumental in getting her married. The daughter of this aunt's neighbour in Kolkata apparently lived in Singapore and that's how the alliance had, in a nutshell, come about. Jhumpa never lost sight of the fact of how bizarre it all was. Apparently, this Kolkata aunt had heard about Salil in what she kept referring to as 'divine providence', during a conversation with her neighbour one afternoon, over tea and *chanachur*.[2]

When Jhumpa had asked what the conversation was about, her aunt brushed it aside and asked her to simply thank her for arranging a rich, handsome and 'foreign' boy for her. She had rather insightfully told Jhumpa: 'These days you get better Bengali foreign boys in Singapore and Dubai than in the States. The boys in America are foolishly marrying white girls! Salil is the right match for

---

[2] An Indian snack mix which consists of a mixture of spicy dried ingredients such as fried lentils, peanuts, chickpeas, corn, flaked rice, fried onion and curry leaves.

you. It's too bad that both his parents died a few years ago. But they were rich and left him a big house. Besides, you don't have to deal with in-laws; now, how fortunate is that?'

Nothing about Salil was 'foreign' except for a slight accent that Jhumpa later attributed to his simply being Singaporean. Salil had an affable demeanour and didn't seem flashy, as how Jhumpa had imagined all NRI bachelors to be. He, however, seemed distracted for someone who had come to meet his possible life partner. He was interrupted constantly by calls and text messages. That he was a bigshot in his bank seemed evident: answering work calls on international roaming rates was the hallmark of someone busy and influential, Jhumpa had reasoned, even if it had assuredly put her off.

Salil had seemed positive about Jhumpa's job prospects in Singapore. 'I can put you on to good headhunters who'll help you land a job. If anything, the finance sector is big and booming in Singapore,' he had assured Jhumpa, who was keen on but nervous about a career abroad. Little did Salil know that her apprehensions had less to do with finding a job and more to do with dealing with the fringe aspects while trying to look for one. Jhumpa worried endlessly about her appearance. What kind of clothes did one wear in Singapore? Did her long, braided hair look shabby? She wanted to talk about all this and more with Salil. But Jhumpa's mother was too busy barraging Salil with questions of her own, not giving Jhumpa a chance to speak. 'Do you get good quality *cha* in Singapore? What about fish?' Jhumpa had watched on in disbelief as her mother proceeded to ask about the price of fish and mutton from an amused Salil. After that conversation, Jhumpa was too mortified to ask more, much less ask questions about her anxieties, lest she appeared a simpleton.

They met a couple more times after that and, each time, Jhumpa wore clothes that were as modern as possible. The first time she met him without being chaperoned, at his hotel's coffee shop, she was wearing jeans with a short, sleeveless *kurti*.[3] Her mother had approved of it. 'Good, good. You must wear more jean pant and *kurti*s. But I hear it's very hot in Singapore. Be sure to get some sleeveless blouses stitched. Salil mentioned there are many Bengalis in Singapore—you can wear saris to their houses when invited.'

Jhumpa liked Salil's grounded nature, but worried how he really was. Her mother had responded to her fears with her personal experience with Jhumpa's father, whom they had lost very early in their lives to an accident. 'Jhumu, marriage is a gamble. I know parents give their children away fully aware of the horrors that lurk around. But life is such that you can only take decisions like these instinctively, there are no guarantees in life. You are educated and smart; if anything goes wrong, you'll have a job and me to fall back on. Your *mashi*[4] has done all the necessary background checks—he seems like a nice boy. Also, her neighbour has told her that Singapore has almost no crime. Isn't that reassuring?'

Jhumpa's mother's definition of a nice boy vastly varied from Jhumpa's idea of a good man, but she also

---

[3] A short tunic worn with jeans, leggings or jeggings.

[4] Maternal aunt.

knew that small-town girls didn't get to reject good proposals based on unfounded fears.

Her mother's first question to Jhumpa over the phone after they had flown the day after their wedding reception was: 'How many Bengalis live near your home, Jhumu?' Her mother worried about her, knowing how shy Jhumpa was.

Every afternoon when they spoke over the phone, her mother would sneak in suggestions: 'What do you mean by how can I just ring their bell? Why don't you make *chorchori*[5] or *roshogolla*[6] and visit your neighbour's house?' Jhumpa would change the subject but would find herself in the same conversation before she knew it the next day. 'I think you must invite them to tea.' 'Did Salil talk to his boss about that job for you?' Jhumpa would eventually get tired and just listen passively while her mother doled out her list of recommendations and questions to which Jhumpa never had any answers.

Jhumpa's life in Jalpaiguri, West Bengal had been fairly ordinary. She wasn't like her friend Sushmita who dreamed of going to Bombay to become an actress nor was she like Mili, her cousin who always wanted to go to America. Jhumpa didn't have dreams like any of her friends. She was a gratified girl who loved the hills, her city, her job as a private bank's assistant branch manager and her assorted bunch of aunts and cousins who lived in close proximity to her family—everything

---

[5] A dry vegetable dish from West Bengal.
[6] A dessert comprising ball-shaped dumplings of cottage cheese and semolina dough, cooked in a light sugary syrup.

else in her life was on the periphery. She had often wondered where she stood in Maslow's hierarchy of needs. She always seemed satisfied with whatever she had in her small world, which is why her frustrations and melancholy made no sense to her after she moved to Singapore.

Jhumpa had looked forward to spending more time with Salil and getting to know him. The way things had moved after the wedding, it seemed like she'd never get around to knowing him at all. Salil had held her hand tightly on their flight to Singapore and explained as much as he could. Those four hours on the flight, she realised later on, would be the crux of her life in Singapore. Salil was a loving guy, but with no time to love. He had told Jhumpa in no uncertain words: 'Life in Singapore will be entirely what you make of it. You have to figure out everything yourself, because I'll be travelling a lot to set up new teams in Southeast Asia. You must find your way around. I will introduce you to my friends whom you can liberally make use of—they are my childhood friends from Singapore, and they'll be happy to help. We'll have a good life, Jhumu,' Salil had endearingly called her, like her mother did.

Jhumpa had questions but didn't ask any, should he think her incapable of taking on a challenge. That the challenge was an entirely new life in a country she knew nothing about, hadn't dawned on her. Introducing her to his childhood friends remained on his to-do list for months. Jhumpa realised soon enough that her Singaporean husband was a workaholic with no social life. He was lovely on days he was relatively less busy, but they were as rare as finding fresh *hilsa* fish[7] in their neighbourhood market.

When Jhumpa met Auntie Chia a few weeks after she had moved into Salil's house, she felt a familiar warm feeling of having met someone from home. Even though Auntie was very busy harvesting some greens that Jhumpa couldn't recognise, she had made Jhumpa feel welcome to Lim Tai See with her chatter. 'The neighbourhood committee head Mr Andrew Chow will soon reach out to you with a welcome basket. Don't miss the papaya, that is from my garden! And the cookies you will get will be from your neighbour Auntie Ann. Everyone calls me Auntie Chia. Uncle *no-mo*.[8] Died two years ago—now I have Princess who is like my daughter, but my real daughter is in Australia. She live there now. Your husband never take walk in Lim Tai See? You his new bride from India, what? What's your name? You have beautiful hair, and your face is lucky.'

Jhumpa had smiled shyly at Auntie Chia who had smiled back endearingly, flashing her dentures. That was the first time she felt somewhat happy in weeks of moving to Singapore. No one had ever called her face 'lucky'. She would learn, over the years, all about lucky faces and unlucky ones in Auntie Chia's esteemed company.

Salil had gone back to work the night after they had landed. He had left a few hundred dollars with a note by her bedside. 'You'll figure it out. Use the Internet

---

[7] *Hilsa* is a kind of herring is fairly common in the Indian subcontinent, particularly West Bengal, but not as much in Southeast Asia.
[8] Singlish for 'no more'.

and Google Maps if you wish to discover the area. For fresh milk and groceries go to FairPrice—call a cab using the app I have downloaded on your phone. Call me if you need anything though I might not answer if I'm in a meeting. I love you and can't wait to have you in my arms.'

For weeks Jhumpa struggled with her new life in Singapore. One morning, exhausted with her own moping, Jhumpa decided to venture out. She still couldn't gather the confidence to call a cab, so she decided to just walk. Jhumpa marvelled at the beautiful houses and clean streets. She didn't come across any stray dogs that she was so accustomed to in Jalpaiguri. She sweated profusely and made a mental note to carry an umbrella the next time she ventured out. She discovered a 7-Eleven that looked like a posh version of Jalpaiguri's Shyamlal and Sons Mini Mart. Entering it, she asked for a packet of fresh milk. They pointed her to a fridge that stocked five varieties of milk in plastic bottles. She picked one with 'full cream' written on it and told the cashier she would return the bottle on her walk the next day. The cashier had stared at her, bewildered.

Then, a little later, in a rather serendipitous turn of events, Jhumpa had found Auntie Chia with a bag on her shoulder and a large shopper on wheels at what looked like a bus stop. That was the beginning of their friendship. Auntie had taken Jhumpa for a spin on bus number 970, showing her their neighbourhood. Jhumpa couldn't have been more grateful for Auntie's display of kindness. When Jhumpa had given the bus driver the $100 bill Salil had left for her, Auntie Chia had asked

Jhumpa to put that away and instead used her extra EZ-Link card, which she gave her to use till she got one of her own. 'You will irritate bus uncle if you give no change. You have too much money, what? Get yourself a bus card, that cheaper *leh*!' Jhumpa's induction into Singapore's public transport couldn't have happened in a more practical way.

Auntie Chia would speak with Jhumpa for hours on end. Though neither understood wholly what the other talked about, they somehow managed to communicate effectively. In a bid to try and show Auntie that she knew much about Chinese food, when Auntie had pointed a local hotpot place to her, Jhumpa told how much she loved American chopsuey and chicken manchurian.[9] Auntie had smiled through her dentures, not understanding anything and had, in turn, told Jhumpa she would one day take her for steamboat. Jhumpa had agreed excitedly to the prospect of going on a ride with Auntie on the Singapore River, not knowing that Auntie was talking about a simmering pot of soup.

Auntie Chia was like Sumita Mashima who lived down the road from Jhumpa's house in Jalpaiguri. Jhumpa missed her the most every evening, for after work Sumita Mashima would bring with her a big box full of hot fried brinjal fritters which she would share over a cup of tea and that day's gossip.

---

[9] American chopsuey and chicken manchurian are savoury dishes in fusion Indian Chinese cuisine. The former is prepared with a sweet and sour thick sauce, stir-fried vegetables and/or meat or chicken over crispy fried noodles, and the latter is comprised of fried chicken balls in a gravy served with Hakka noodles or fried rice.

Auntie Chia became Jhumpa's GPS, tour guide and local guardian. It was an unusual friendship that blossomed between the two. Auntie had not just shown Jhumpa where to shop and what to eat, she had also taught Jhumpa how not to get fleeced by wet-market vendors and how to shop using a smattering of Hokkien and Singlish.

But the greatest gift that Jhumpa received from Auntie Chia was her love for gardening. It was through Auntie Chia that Jhumpa realised how much she enjoyed digging, weeding and pruning. Jhumpa had grown up watching her mother plant chilli, pumpkin, bitter gourd and Malabar spinach alongside the seasonal petunias, roses, gerberas, dahlias and her favourite, marigold, in their garden. Come October, their garden burst into a riot of colours. The memory always came alive in Jhumpa's mind, making her wistful for a home that she found hard to let go of. She held the scent of *genda*[10] in her heart like a memento.

Auntie Chia went on to suggest other places of interest around the neighbourhood along with Hoon San Temple.

'Auntie, I'll visit the temple someday soon, but today I have come to help you. I would love to help you clear out the patch in front of House 11. Maybe we can plant flowers there?' Jhumpa was keen on helping out and making something of her otherwise boring days. She had bookmarked jobs on the Internet she thought she was qualified for and had applied to them before reciting a little prayer to Ma Durga. She fervently hoped to get a

---

[10] Marigold in Hindi.

call, while also Googling 'appropriate clothes to wear to work in Singapore'.

'Oh! You *wan*[11] to help? Sure, can do. Here, take this and start clearing out the grass first,' Auntie Chia said, handing Jhumpa a pair of gardening gloves.

Delighted, Jhumpa set to work and began pulling out the grass, weeds and creepers that had taken over the entire space. It was therapeutic to say the least—she huffed and puffed but enjoyed every moment of it. The dirt in her hands, the smell of grass mingled with sweat trickling down her forehead and armpits made her feel like a consummate gardener.

Over the next few days, Auntie Chia and Jhumpa cleared the entire patch of overgrown land, loosened the soil and got it ready to sow seeds. They then waited for saplings, which they would replant alongside the entire Lim Tai See Walk. They had grand plans.

'What variety of flowers are these?' Jhumpa asked. She knew more about flowers than vegetables and wondered if she would recognise the name. While Jhumpa truly loved heliconias and ginger flowers, her heart coveted the scent of flowers from her childhood.

'I don't remember, Joopa. My sister sent these seeds through my brother-in-law yesterday. Remember I told you about her? She lives in Choa Chu Kang and has a big flower garden. These seeds I think are from her garden flowers. These could be daisies or maybe marigold. Most likely daisy.'

After a long day of work Auntie Chia invited Jhumpa to her home for a cup of tea. Jhumpa had grown

---

[11] 'Want' in Singlish.

surprisingly fond of *teh tarik*,[12] something tea snobs never did. The cloyingly sweet, condensed milk in the *teh* perhaps appealed to Jhumpa's Bengali tastebuds. But she figured early on that it wasn't good for her waistline. She instead requested Auntie for *teh-O-kosong*, which was simply black tea or liquor *cha*.

'You so good with gardening, Joopa ... I'm so happy you helped. If you keep your head down and just grow your own food and plant flowers for all to enjoy, your life will be easy in Singapore. You will miss home a little less.' Auntie Chia's words surprised Jhumpa. Until then she hadn't realised that her loneliness and anguish was manifestly perceptible. She made a mental note to appear more cheerful, at least for Auntie Chia's sake.

That evening Jhumpa got home and cooked a big meal. Salil was pleased with the array of dishes on the dining table—from his favourite *chorchori* to *kangkong*[13] stir fry and her freshly learned recipe of Nyonya fish head curry,[14] Jhumpa had gone all out. She spoke lovingly of Auntie Chia to Salil. Salil was delighted that Jhumpa was making an effort to familiarise herself with the neighbours. He told her about how difficult it was to set up a team in their Hong Kong office and his hurdles within the company. They chatted about banking and Salil let her into some investments he had made.

---

[12] A hot milk tea beverage, it is a strong brew of black tea blended with condensed milk, commonly found in *kopitiam*s or traditional coffeeshops in Singapore, Malaysia and Indonesia.

[13] Water spinach or Chinese spinach.

[14] Nyonya cuisine comes from the Peranakans, descendants of early Chinese migrants who settled in Penang, Malacca, Singapore and Indonesia and intermarried with local Malays.

Together they spoke about each other's days and there was something satisfying about that. Jhumpa shared with Salil her trials with her job applications and he apologised for not having introduced her to the headhunters. 'That's alright, will you instead invite your childhood friends over for dinner one of these days when you are home and not travelling?' Jhumpa had suggested. Increasingly Jhumpa was getting more and more into the groove, not giving in to nagging voices in her head about her being a misfit. That night she slept contentedly, a feeling that had eluded her since her move to the island city-state.

Salil's phone rang at 6 am the next morning, an unknown number from India flashing on the screen. He was irritated and almost cancelled the call before reluctantly answering it. A sobbing voice informed Salil of Jhumpa's mother's demise. It was Jhumpa's aunt. Jhumpa's mother had died of a heart attack. While delivering the news, her aunt had also told Salil to tell Jhumpa not to come for the funeral—they had already cremated her and, on Jhumpa's mother's last wish, had not informed Jhumpa earlier. Her mother didn't wish to disturb the newly-weds' life. She also did not want Jhumpa to fuss over her last rites—Jhumpa could do it to appease herself in Singapore in a temple, when convenient. Ever so practical, even in her death, Jhumpa's mother ensured no one was inconvenienced. She had raised Jhumpa as a single mother and had always kept their lives uncomplicated and happy.

When Jhumpa heard the news, she was devastated. It all seemed unreal. She was angry that her mother had robbed her of her right to see her one last time. Her mother was the only living member of her immediate family, the only connection she had with Jalpaiguri. Her aunts, uncles and cousins were but distant relatives after all. The realisation that she had effectively lost all ties to the one place she called home dawned on her.

Jhumpa isolated herself from everything. Salil had tried to evade his trip to the United States but couldn't. He would be gone for a month. He worried for Jhumpa but knew, having dealt with his parents' loss, that this was a kind of grief one had to suffer and make peace with on one's own. One had to take solace in the fact that while with a parent's death a light extinguishes inside one, a part of them lives on through one as well. He left Jhumpa with an embrace and a kiss on her forehead. 'Take care and text me as much as you can.' Salil's words were barely audible to Jhumpa.

With Salil gone, Jhumpa became a recluse and never stepped out for anything. She missed speaking with her mother in the afternoons and yearned to hear her suggestions. She broke down at little things that even remotely reminded her of her mother. The pumpkin creeper she had sown had crept all the way up to her bedroom window and was full of pumpkin flowers. This would have otherwise brought Jhumpa immense joy, had it not reminded her of how her mother made fritters of them for Jhumpa. Salil called often but Jhumpa always hung up after a few minutes. If she tried suppressing her mother's memories, she'd think about the house in Jalpaiguri. What would become of her home? Her aunt had suggested they sell it, but Jhumpa was aghast at her proposal. It was, after all, the only place she could find vestiges of her childhood.

This went on for weeks. Jhumpa grieved over not just losing a mother, but also a forever home.

Then, one morning, Jhumpa woke up to the doorbell ringing incessantly. Despite herself, she went to the window to see Auntie Chia outside. Jhumpa wasn't ready to meet anyone but Auntie Chia was looking up straight at her bedroom window, waving. Jhumpa felt ashamed. She had never once thought of sending word to her. She splashed water onto her face and hurried down to open the gate, expecting Auntie Chia to be upset.

'Look, Joopa, I got you some *di gua mio cari* ... you know, yam leaves? Remember we planted them? This is your hard work, Joopa. And Joopa ... I'm very sorry about your mother. Your husband told me the night before he left for America. He came home and asked me to take care of you. But I knew how you were feeling, I have also lost my husband. I know the pain. So, I decide to let you cry as much as you can. But now, enough already. Freshen up and eat this. This is called the longevity vegetable, it will give you strength. It is also anti-cancer!' Auntie Chia smiled infectiously.

Jhumpa smiled sadly, grateful for Auntie's endless kindness, but couldn't bring herself to speak.

'Okay I go now, but I'll see you tomorrow morning; my old knees need help, Joopa. The patch opposite House 12 has long long one grass. You better come,' Auntie lightheartedly threatened.

Jhumpa had her first proper meal in days. She took the day to gather herself and face the life she had ahead of her without her mother, without Jalpaiguri, without a home. What was the meaning of home anyway, Jhumpa reasoned. For Jhumpa home was a place with her people, a place where she spoke a common language, walked known roads and met familiar people. Home was the smell of roasted tealeaves, hanging clouds and festivals, and now she no longer had that. If she could somehow learn to live with this knowledge, she knew life would get less difficult.

Next morning, she woke up to a koel. She thought she was dreaming, but she went closer to the window and opened it to a *coooo*! The call was unmistakable. She wondered how the mynahs were doing. After her cup of *cha*, she opened her gate after a month. Daylight made her squint. She decided to stroll all the way from the beginning of Lim Tai See to the end, where she would find Auntie Chia. As she looked on, she was caught unawares, it was a sight to behold. Lim Tai See Walk was flanked on either side with blooming marigolds. Jhumpa stood in the middle of the road with tears of joy and grief gleaming in her eyes, not believing the uncanny timing of the blooms.

Auntie Chia appeared from behind her and said joyously, 'Remember these, Joopa? These are the seeds from my sister's garden that we had sown. They turned out to be marigold. See how they seem to be welcoming you?'

Overwhelmed with feelings of an insight her heart had just deduced, Jhumpa hugged Auntie Chia.

'I think you should go home for a while, Joopa,' Auntie Chia said tenderly.

'I *am* home, Auntie! Home is where the marigolds are,' Jhumpa said as hugged her tighter. She felt lighter, as light as the clouds that drifted over her head when she ran down the rickety roads of Jalpaiguri.

She went home and texted Salil, 'I felt and smelt Mother on Lim Tai See today.' Salil read on, perplexed.

A few days later, Auntie Chia and Jhumpa visited Hoon San temple to offer prayers to Jhumpa's ancestors and mother.

8

Memsahib

Ranjani Rao

'You have become a *memsahib*,'[1] Seema said with a laugh. *Memsahib*!

When was the last time I had heard this quaint word—usually found in conjunction with colonial-era English literature—in casual conversation?

Seema and I usually caught up on WhatsApp calls on weekdays between noon and 1 pm when she drove back after teaching her yoga class in Perth, and I strolled around Biopolis after a quick solitary lunch in my office. Despite a distance of 4,000 kilometres, we were in the same time zone. In the digital age, distance didn't count. Connectivity was the key for connection.

Despite our many differences, we had one thing in common. After long marriages that had ended in divorce, we had both remarried in midlife and embarked on our second innings in two different countries.

Our lives in Australia and Singapore were as different as the countries themselves. Seema lived in a large house with a yard and watched her husband interact with his two teenage sons on weekends. My daughter and I moved into a condominium that overlooked Bukit Timah Hill with my new husband and his young daughter.

---

[1] A married foreign woman of upper-class status.

While Seema drove long distances on the wide-open highways of Australia, I travelled by bus and train across Singapore, reminiscing about my growing-up years in Mumbai, or Bombay, as it was known then.

Life in Mumbai had meant home was a cramped apartment shared with my two brothers, my parents and, later, a grandmother. From our house in the suburbs, my father travelled by crowded local trains to his office in South Bombay. Amma had an even more gruelling daily routine that included cooking and caring for a family, a job that did not pay a salary or let her have time off.

Meri beti aaj kya khayegi?[2] Amma would ask me on Sunday mornings. Although the line was plagiarised from a TV advertisement for a popular brand of cooking oil, at twelve, I loved being included in such a major decision. Depending on my response, she would prepare my favourite foods—sometimes fried treats, other times simple, wholesome meals.

Although Amma had graduated from college with a degree in mathematics, she seemed content to be a homemaker. Her most important job was to feed her ravenous family. When our widowed maternal grandmother moved in with us, our male-majority family of five grew to a total of six, with an even number of males and females.

Everyone was responsible for keeping their own assigned nooks for clothes and books tidy, but cooking was the one area in which the lines were severely drawn along gendered lines.

---

[2] What will my daughter eat today?

On any given day, Amma and Aji would be in the kitchen from the early hours of the morning: brewing coffee, making breakfast, packing lunch boxes. They managed everything, from drawing up monthly lists of kitchen staples to daily menu planning. They sourced fresh ingredients, chopped vegetables, ground spices and cooked multiple warm, nourishing meals. Day. After. Day.

In the extended family, although my father's sisters worked outside the home, they still bore the primary responsibility for cooking in their own homes, with or without the help of part-time maids who assisted with meal prep or showed up in time to make chapattis for lunch or dinner.

This inequity bothered me even as a young girl. Displeased by the unfairness, I argued with Amma, the only person who engaged with my bold views and rigid stances.

Are you asking me to fold clothes just because I am a girl?

How come I got less of the carrot halwa[3] *that you made?*

Why should I help with peeling the potatoes? Why don't you ask your sons?

I saw everything through a gendered lens, convinced that I was getting a raw deal, whether that meant being given more chores or a smaller share of treats.

Amma always listened. Unfazed by my impertinence and guided by an unwavering sense of justice, she would patiently respond to each of my questions.

I asked you because you are better at this task. Even in a job, you will find that people who do better work are given more assignments.

---

[3] A sweet Indian dish consisting of carrots or semolina boiled with milk, almonds, sugar, butter and cardamom.

Your brother ate more halwa *because he grated more carrots—the three of you agreed to the deal.*

I like to chat with you while we peel potatoes.

Amma was right. She was always fair when it came to distributing tasks inside the house or sending us out on errands. I didn't like grating carrots, even though I loved carrot *halwa.* And I hung out with her in the kitchen because that is where she spent most of her time.

During sultry Mumbai summers I learnt to fry fluffy balloon-like *poori*s[4] best enjoyed with *aamras.*[5] On cool evenings, I tried making crisp, round *dosa*s,[6] taking on the challenge of ensuring that each one was perfectly circular and uniformly golden. I practised making round chapattis,[7] despite disparaging comments from my brothers who compared the weird shapes of my early attempts with the maps of various countries, instigating a chase around the kitchen with a rolling pin.

Over time, I developed into a competent sous chef. But I showed no interest in learning how to cook independently.

'She will learn cooking when she needs to. She learns everything quickly. It's not that difficult,' Amma would assure nosy relatives who ignored my stellar grades in college but enquired about my expertise in the kitchen.

---

[4] An Indian wholewheat bread formed in flat rounds of dough that puff up when deep fried.

[5] A thick, sweet concoction made with the pulp of juicy Alphonso mangoes.

[6] A type of thin south Indian pancake made from fermented lentils and rice blended with water.

[7] A round, flat unleavened Indian bread that is usually made of wholewheat flour and cooked on a griddle.

When I became the first among my siblings to leave India, to drive a car and to obtain a PhD, I broke many stereotypes. Yet the one barrier I could not overcome was the prerequisite for 'homely' girls—an aptitude for cooking. Amma's prophecy, however, did come true.

Soon after moving to America as a young bride, I learnt to cook. I became an efficient cook, if not an imaginative one. To minimise time in the kitchen, I began to use a microwave and rice cooker—not just the Prestige pressure cooker, the standard staple of Indian kitchens that had accompanied me to America. I bought frozen vegetables and canned chickpeas and concocted one-pot recipes. Soon I could put together a full Indian meal within forty-five minutes. This skill, coupled with a dishwasher to help with the cleanup, gave me time to do other things: watch *Friends*, read or write.

Even as I took on responsibilities, first as a research scientist and then as a mother, I was unable to relinquish my role in the kitchen, a point that never came up in discussion.

The act of cooking was straightforward but the associated burden of stocking the pantry and the fridge, giving thought to every single meal—whether eaten within or outside the house—the process of planning, execution and cleanup, was a major energy suck that got on my nerves with each passing year. I resented having to bear the burden of feeding my family solely because I was a woman.

Until my divorce.

Breaking social conventions sometimes leads to unexpected side effects.

I had moved back to India by the time my marriage dissolved. To my surprise, divorce freed me from kitchen duties, not just a dysfunctional marital relationship.

I was still a mother, though. And a person who preferred to eat at home.

I eschewed instant noodles and packaged foods, preferring instead to whip up simple meals from scratch—*aloo paratha*s[8] with pickle, vegetable *pulao*[9] with yogurt *raita*,[10] hearty pasta and stuffed sandwiches. Easy to prepare, quick to assemble.

Life, stripped to the bare essentials, was beautiful.

The well-paying job that allowed me to be financially independent as a single parent, however, turned out to be a boon and a curse. Without family support and reliable after-school care, my eight-year-old daughter had to stay alone at home for hours until I returned after a long day at the office.

I had to choose between earning money for financial security versus staying home for my child's physical safety. No job title, promotion or perks could compensate for the peace of mind I gained by being home when she got back from school.

The laughable myth that women could 'have it all' had never felt like a bigger joke. I scaled down my

---

[8] Lit. potato *paratha* is a bread dish originating from the Indian subcontinent. It consists of unleavened dough rolled with a mixture of mashed potato and spices, which is cooked on a hot griddle with butter or ghee.

[9] A rice dish whose recipe usually involves cooking in stock or broth, adding spices and other ingredients such as vegetables or meat.

[10] An Indian side dish made of yogurt, with diced vegetables and seasonings.

expenses, sought freelance work and managed to keep the home fires burning.

Years later, when I met Aditya, a kindred spirit and a widower with a young child, we thought deeply before jumping into matrimony and agreeing to begin our new life in Singapore. I looked forward to once again being part of a 'regular' family. This time I hoped to have an equal marriage in which we shared our daily details and pursued common goals while guiding our children as a united parental unit.

After walking around the sacred fire, as we were showered with rice grains as blessings, I wondered if I would once again have to wrestle with the rice cooker. Why did women always have to bear the responsibility of feeding their family?

When we arrived in Singapore, I was unsure if I would become a contemporary version of my aunts, torn between work and home, or a watered-down version of my mother given my lack of dedication to the kitchen.

Fortunately, there was no struggle. Thanks to Maria.

The reason Seema called me *memsahib*.

Maria, a young woman from the Philippines, was our helper. The Ministry of Manpower termed her a Foreign Domestic Worker. Like us, she had left behind her home country to find employment in Singapore. Unlike us, a newly blended family, she had come alone, leaving behind her three children in Manila. While she lived and worked in our household six days a week, taking Sundays off as per the standard contract terms, her children were being brought up by her siblings.

Before our move, when Aditya had suggested hiring a live-in helper, I had balked at the idea. I had never had such help. Through my childhood in Mumbai, a maid came in daily to wash the dishes and sweep. In the US, I had done the cleaning and vacuuming.

In Singapore, I was already worried about the difficulty of weaving together our family given the circumstances of our union. Did I really want to add another person to the mix?

'Having a live-in maid is common here. Most of my friends, especially those with kids, have one. Once you start working, it will make a big difference,' Aditya tried to convince me.

'Can we afford this?' I asked.

'We will manage,' he replied confidently. I wasn't so sure.

Within a few weeks of our arrival, Maria joined us, fully trained and mentally prepared to complete her required two-year contract. It was her second stint in Singapore. She knew what her job entailed. I didn't.

We spent the first few weeks setting up the house, arranging and rearranging the furniture and organising the kitchen. Every week we headed to the local market to stock up on groceries and household essentials. Maria had a preference for a broom (not plastic), wet mop (a bucket with a side panel for easy wringing) and dishwashing detergent (Joy, she was allergic to Mama Lemon). She knew which stores had the best fruit and cheapest deals on everything from toilet paper to Snickers bars. Her comfort in handling the shopping trolley and familiarity with the market made it easier for me to settle in.

I labelled plastic storage containers with the names of various dals[11] and spices essential to Indian kitchens.

---

[11] Lentils.

Within a few days, Maria learnt to cook basic Indian meals. She diligently recorded every recipe in her notebook, using a mix of English and Tagalog.

'Oh, my *gulay*!'[12] She often exclaimed, as she put away the vegetables after an afternoon at the market.

I taught her to make *labanos*[13] *sambar*[14] and *kamatis*[15] *rasam*,[16] which she learnt rapidly. The ease and speed with which she mastered the art of making round chapattis and crisp *dosa*s astonished me.

Our family of four had varied food preferences. While Aditya and I preferred regular desi *khana*,[17] our kids loved pizza, pasta and *paneer*.[18] Maria and I pored over YouTube videos and old cookbooks that had accompanied me from India to the US and now to Singapore.

Maria went about her activities with a big smile, singing as she scrubbed toilets, exclaiming loudly when it rained right after she had cleaned the glass windows. Her enthusiastic presence was the one bright spot in the lonely initial months when I waited for my family to return: from work, from school, from the exciting lives they led outside the walls of our home while I feverishly applied for jobs.

Maria's help was exactly what I needed as I integrated myself back into a traditional family system after a brief

---

[12] A Filipino word that means 'vegetables'.

[13] Radish.

[14] A lentil-based stew with vegetables.

[15] Tomato.

[16] A south Indian soup, traditionally prepared using tamarind juice as a base.

[17] Food.

[18] Cottage cheese.

spell of single parenthood. It had been what I had needed all along. Her energy and focus on the mundane but necessary details of family life liberated me from expending energy on cooking and cleaning. Her presence allowed me to have the brain space and bandwidth needed to engage with the people in my life without being exhausted and depleted as I had always been for all the years of my adult life. But this relief came at a cost.

With two kids in private schools, running the household on one salary was not easy. Our assumption that I would find employment in no time, given my educational credentials and international work experience, had not panned out. I had fiercely valued financial independence, but I was now uncomfortably dependent on my husband. Not only was I letting the family down by not contributing financially, I was also disappointing myself.

I had become a *memsahib*.

Maria's lively personality made me smile. But her mere presence was a daily reminder of my decadent life as a 'homemaker', a term that didn't sit very well on my lips.

I felt the true impact of Maria's contribution when I finally found a job that required me to be at the office five days a week. I took the bus and train to work, like my aunts had done back in the day. Except I could leave home without worrying about the meals that needed to be cooked, clothes that needed washing and rooms that required cleaning. Maria did all that.

Our family of four functioned on the foundation of Maria's support. While I still made grocery lists and discussed mealtimes and menus, I didn't have to personally pack school lunches or peel peas during my commute, a common sight in the ladies' compartment in Mumbai local trains.

For the first time in my working life, I had the exact support I needed to be able to function freely at work and at home. My attention was no longer splintered into tiny shards that clouded my vision. My children were older and not needy, my house was clean and clutter-free, and there was a hot meal on the table when we all got home.

In the words of Pulitzer-Prize winning *Washington Post* journalist Brigid Schulte, 'Women's time has been interrupted and fragmented throughout history, the rhythms of their days circumscribed by the Sisyphean tasks of housework, childcare and kin work—keeping family and community ties strong.'[19] No matter how much progress society makes, the deficiency of time is an affliction that unfairly targets women.

I had become a *memsahib* because of one choice— to move to Singapore where I could exercise another choice—to formally hire domestic help in a well-thought-out system. My ease and ability to move in the direction of personal growth was built on the labour of another woman.

In all fairness, Maria and I both worked: she, inside my home, and me, outside it. We both wanted the same things—financial security for ourselves, a better future for our kids and, above all, to be self-sufficient.

---

[19] Brigid Schulte, 'A Woman's Greatest Enemy? A Lack of Time to Herself', *The Guardian*, 21 July 2019, https://www.theguardian.com/commentisfree/2019/jul/21/woman-greatest-enemy-lack-of-time-themselves [accessed 24 December 2020].

Maria took care of the minutiae of my life. I watched over her overall wellbeing.

While Maria bore the pain of separation from her family, I took on the responsibility of adding her to mine. I monitored her health and her moods. I accompanied her to the doctor for minor illnesses and consulted with my doctor friends to get to the root of her persistent headaches, later diagnosed as high blood pressure, a family trait that Maria had not disclosed.

Maria's ability to be easily influenced by her friends frequently got her into trouble. She once bought a special coffee that held the promise of weight loss. She developed an ulcer instead. From one look at her face, I could tell what kind of a day she had had, whether it was an unpleasant call from home or a case of indigestion.

There were days when I wondered if my daughters were learning the right lessons by watching Maria who made their beds and laid out perfectly presented meals. Unable to cook, unwilling to clean and maintain their living spaces, would they be empowered women outside but helpless within their own homes?

And then there were times when I looked back at the army of women who had helped me thus far: my mother who had burped my newborn at night so I could rest, the babysitter who had cared for my child in California during the week, the neighbour who had sent over snacks to my teenage daughter on the days I arrived late from meetings during my years as a single parent in India.

What I had needed was what women have always needed—support, regardless of whether it came from loving relatives, considerate friends or paid help. I had been fortunate to have had sufficient financial and social capital to cobble together a network to hold me up. Maria was the latest in a long line of facilitators.

As we came together over meals and boardgames, TV shows and strolls around our neighbourhood, Maria embedded herself into the fabric of our family life. I hope that one day my daughters will weave a rich tapestry of their own.

9

A Room of Our Own

Kalpana Mohan

I stayed up late into the night on days when the quotidian chores of the morning sucked out all my words. Mostly, though, I wrote from morning to night. I left the bedroom door unlocked as I worked, aware that I was occupying space once claimed by my sister's grandson who was all of seven. Several times a day, Vedoo's cherubic face popped into my room.

Vedoo always tended to sulk a little, as if life weren't wholly perfect, but he managed to dish out a smile or giggle in between and when he smiled, he did so with his mouth, his eyes and his forehead—with the light of a thousand suns. He trudged into the room with his toys, asking the same question at least once a day. 'Heeeyyy, why are you writing all the time?' At other times he asked me if I was finished with my book, a memoir about his recently deceased great-grandfather.

Vedoo had every reason to be a little peeved. As long as I was working I occupied his space, having taken possession of it during my twelve-day vacation. Naturally, he came in to plant himself beneath the window of my room so as to re-establish control of his dominion—forthrightly a few times, and disingenuously at other times—stating that he had originally conquered this 80-square-foot space called a spare bedroom when he had first arrived at the end of May. As such, given that

I had arrived much later, in July, the room really belonged to him and not to me. His sudden cameo appearances were small, pointed inroads at reclaiming land that belonged to him.

The notion of land reclamation was fitting in my sister's residence. We were in Singapore, after all, an island-state of which more than a quarter of the area has been reclaimed from the sea. Fifteen floors below us unfurled the black ribbon of Tanjong Rhu Road that connected the airport to the periphery of the old town. My sister and brother-in-law's apartment rose in what used to be the old shipyard of Singapore. The name 'Tanjon Rû' harks back to sixteenth-century Singapore when Manuel Godinho de Erédia, a cartographer on a Portuguese expedition in search of new lands, marked it on his map of the island. For several hundred years Singapore would remain unclaimed by European powers until the early part of the nineteenth century when the island assumed special significance under Sir Stamford Raffles, a colonial agent for the British empire. In the early part of the nineteenth century, shipbuilding companies set up shop on the island's coastline that now sprawled out in front of me. This was a magnificent sight from the gargantuan windows that walled me and my extended family into a newly minted extended togetherness.

Our family had entered a fresh phase of life that June. My sister and I had just lost our ninety-year-old father who had lived in Chennai. After the completion of the thirteen days of rites as per Hindu custom my sister flew back to Singapore, where her grandchildren eagerly awaited her return. They had flown down from the United States for their annual summer holidays. When my sister and brother-in-law suggested that I too should fly out from Chennai to stay with them for a while, I had lodged a feeble protest. I wanted to remain in our parents' home in Chennai and continue working on my book, the last chapter of which I had not yet begun. But they would have none of it. My brother-in-law flew me out to their home by the waters and so there I was, in the middle of it all, sandwiched between two senior citizens and two children who didn't clearly understand how the death of a second parent rearranged one's interior. Thus, we were now five of us squeezed into an airy apartment.

Many times, through the course of the day, the five of us seemed to be curled up into ourselves. I was in my bedroom working all day. My brother-in-law could often be found in the living room, an ear stuck to the phone, fielding business calls from India. My sister was either in the kitchen or in front of the television watching a melodrama unfold on an Indian soap channel. Vedoo mostly played in a corner of the living room where his toys only seemed to multiply, thanks to his generous grandparents. On most mornings, my eleven-year-old grandniece Anvi, Vedoo's sister, lounged on the sofa like a girl in a Botticelli painting, confident that her grandfather, my brother-in-law, would always do her bidding.

He was a brusque man of few words who bossed over many at his work in India. In his Singapore home, however, he had morphed into a minion to his two grandchildren who had him wrapped around their twenty little fingers. He was now the worker bee, the man who made his apartment chug like clockwork. His life revolved around ensuring that his grandchildren would never be sad, the way his underlings in Chennai orbited around him fretting that he should never be displeased. In his Singapore avatar, my brother-in-law drove his own car, washed and immaculately folded the laundry, emptied the dishwasher and shopped for groceries. In his alternate life in Chennai, his elderly mother hovered over him. Even though she was now too frail to physically attend to his needs, a designated crew of people ferried him around, cooked his favourite dishes, washed and ironed his clothes and carried out all his commands.

The stark role reversal amused me. I saw a patient grandfather who never lost his temper. 'Shall I make you tofu with salt and pepper, *kanna*?'[1] he asked when one of his grandchildren whined about something or other. 'How about I cut you some fruit?' This large-hearted provider to his extended family now dashed in and out of the kitchen—a territory my sister had conveniently turned over to him—melting butter on toast or sprinkling oil around a *dosa*[2] that Vedoo and Anvi (and I) enjoyed because he was both patient and fastidious in the kitchen.

I was fast becoming another of my brother-in-law's overlords. A snack he was making for his grandchild smelt just right for me too. All three of us loved his braised tofu doused in pepper and salt. Sometimes my brother-in-law brought me a plate of warm samosas[3] with green chutney all the way to my bed where I sat working, pillows bolstering my back, laptop in front of me.

---

[1] Endearment for a child, referring literally to the child avatar of Lord Krishna.

[2] A savoury Indian pancake.

[3] A small triangular pastry filled with spiced meat or vegetables and fried in ghee or oil.

Just as my sister and brother-in-law were preoccupied with their grandchildren between work, I too found myself listening to their stories about the perceived trials and tribulations of their lives. Their view of the world was circumscribed by the things consequential to them: their daily swimming classes, the worlds inside their iPads, their evening tennis lessons, their favourite foods and their clashes over sofa space. On some evenings, the five of us went to the mall to check out a store the children wanted to visit or eat at a restaurant my brother-in-law knew the two of them loved. In between their angst-ridden dialogues and rants at home or in the car, they expressed some genuine concerns about their lives. Anvi worried about grades and subjects. Vedoo shared his frustrations about the bullies at his school. To my ears, I sounded more objective and more constructive than I had ever been with my own children.

The spectre of my father lurked in the corners of my sister's home. Memories of him crept into the conversations I had with the grandchildren and the grandparents. One afternoon during lunch, my brother-in-law reminisced aloud about what my father's departure from the world signified in the trajectory of his businesses. My father had been a figurehead, the philosophical 'glue' to the ventures that his son-in-law had envisioned and built. I began to realise, as he talked, that my father's exit from the world had hastened the slow unravelling of his own work. My father's passing had given us pause. We didn't say it out loud, but I know that the three adults were thinking about the years that we each had left. We were grieving together for the loss of something in our lives that we were, for now, managing to fill with the sound of needy children and the humdrum exigencies of life.

Anvi and Vedoo were too young to understand. Losing just one of my parents was unsettling. Losing both was terrifying. When our father passed away, my sister comforted me. She held me close. I would always have a home to go to in Singapore, she said, reassuring me that she'd always be there for me. But what was 'always'? Our parents had just established that the only truth was the impermanence of life. In an objective sense, it seemed ludicrous that I should feel derailed. Yet there I was, a grown woman of fifty-three with two grown children of my own, my eyes welling up at the oddest times of day. My sister and I had wanted my father's suffering to end, yet the loss felt colossal whenever the memory of a time with both my parents rolled into my mind like a grey cloud on a summer day.

I know my sister struggled, too, even though the care of her grandchildren was a welcome interlude in the aftermath of our father's demise. After each of our parents passed away, she said that mornings were the hardest for her. I figured that the memory of her daily 7 am call to them hung in the air like the odour of a damp, mouldy sponge. I suppose if mourning itself could be quantified in some way, it would be counted by memories and rated, perhaps, by smells and aromas. The sharp tang of an incense stick described the scent of our father. Sandalwood on skin—I call that an incantation to recall the faint scent of our mother. A sliver of mango with drizzled honey—another incantation conjuring my father's face in the recesses of my mind.

I never tried talking to Anvi or Vedoo about loss. I call myself a writer. Yet I couldn't marshal the vocabulary to describe to a child the pain of recall and regret. How would I explain to a little one of seven that the day a part of me died was the summer day—eight years before my father's demise—when my mother inhaled for one last time? How could my sister discipline a child throwing a tantrum that there were far greater crosses to bear and that some wrongs would never be righted—ever? How could I expect my grandniece to understand that the books that I bought her would come in handy in a way that an outfit at the mall never would, that books have a way of filling holes and repairing cracks inside us that are made by the disappearance of a parent? How did anyone explain to two young ones that the presence of a parent, however old, was reassuring because someone, however far away, was worrying about us so *we* didn't have to, as much? Instead, the three adults in our home pretended that life was normal, that the death of a parent was a blip that all humans worked around so that we could hobble onwards in our lives.

For my part, I simply let my sister and brother-in-law's care and attention wash over me during that Singapore stay. They had assumed the burden my parents had bequeathed them—the onus of worrying about their younger child—and they bore it with a fealty and care that in itself was a teachable tale of how family members must support one another. I'd always been grateful for my sister's kindness and compassion although I never thought to say it out aloud to her. I felt entitled to it although I'll admit I'm annoyed when she clucks around me too much. At other times I love it so much that I wish it to be so forever. I suppose this will always be the eternal paradox of intimate relationships. Love is comforting. But too much love feels like a teaspoon of condensed, sweetened milk. You can only ingest so much of it. If love were sold in a can, it would bear a warning that too much of it is perilous to both one's sanity and one's internal drive.

It wasn't the ideal situation for someone working on a deadline, yet this stay in Singapore was somehow loaded with meaning for me. Singapore had always been the place where my husband and I renewed ourselves en route from California to India to see our parents. Until my sister moved there thirty years ago, we landed at Changi Airport in Singapore for a layover after a long flight, staying in a day-use hotel room. After a nine-hour rest, we flew onwards to India. When my sister and brother-in-law made Singapore their home more than two decades ago, their house became the transit haven that our family took for granted. It became a home to which I felt entitled—a piece of land carved out of a world faraway that I too could claim as my own—just as it now was for two vacationing grandchildren who didn't quite fathom the depths of the hollowness which their grandaunt felt in the weeks following their great-grandfather's death.

But it was somewhere in this insensitivity and lack of understanding, in the space that often represents a free fall, that I believe I also found my moorings. For that amount of time and in that space, I was also building, for twelve full days, memories with the next generation in my family. I was reaching outside of myself and leaving my own larger cares. I was entering the world of pre-teens and their precious peeves. On and off I irritated Anvi and Vedoo as much as they exasperated me, but we grew fond of each other in the way family members do who cannot live with—or without—one another. Spending time with the two children and spoiling them as much as we possibly could comforted us adults in ways we hardly comprehended.

Midway through my stay, I spent two mornings and a night with a dear old friend who lived near the Singapore Botanic Gardens. The afternoon I returned to my sister's place the door of the elevator glided open. Vedoo was waiting outside, despair and anticipation creasing his forehead. As soon as I stepped out, he ran back towards the apartment, beaming with delight, his cheeks the colour of a ripe Kashmiri apple.

I ran behind him to squeeze him in a bear hug which he resisted in a fit of giggles. In that moment, one thing was clear. He had missed me almost as much as I had missed him. As I made my way back to my room inside my sister's house, Vedoo and I both knew that his room was also mine now—*almost* as much as it was his.

10

Aaji's Vicissitudes

Payal Morankar

Shuffling of slippers, clinking of bangles, sizzling of curry leaves, and *'Kuch sust kadam raste, kuch tez kadam raahein'*[1] playing softly on a Nokia 3110: these were the only sounds that Mrs Gadkar could hear. She winced every time her spoon clanged against the vessel and disturbed the uncharacteristic silence.

'Good morning, Aaji!' said Leena, hugging her grandmother from behind.

'You've woken up?' said Mrs Gadkar, running her hand over Leena's cheek. 'I'm making *pohe*.[2] What time did you sleep last night?'

'Around 2 am,' said Leena, as she slumped down on a chair beside the kitchen platform.

'What were you doing up so late?'

'Just watching some cocktail tutorials.'

Mrs Gadkar's spoon slipped slightly. 'Yes, that hobby of hers. Bartending!' she scoffed to herself. 'Why don't you learn new dishes from me instead, now?' she asked aloud.

---

[1] An acclaimed song from the Bollywood movie *Aandhi* (1975), the lyrics of which are penned by Gulzar. This line highlights that at a crossroads, we need to choose between a leisurely or fast-paced path. These roads are a metaphor for one's approach to life. In subsequent lines, the lyricist expresses the desire to take whichever path leads to one's beloved.

[2] Flat rice.

'Meh.'

Mrs Gadkar looked up from the vessel to see Leena engrossed in her phone. 'The lockdown may have started today to curb COVID-19, but it is these smartphones that are the true virus. They should be locked up somewhere too!' continued her inner rant.

'Don't start using the phone the minute you wake up,' chided Mrs Gadkar, as she handed Leena a bowl of steaming *pohe*. 'Concentrate on the food when you eat.'

'Baba messaged. He is doing fine there. He got your visa extended. So now you can stay with me for longer,' she grinned.

Mrs Gadkar couldn't help but smile back. The last time she had seen her granddaughter in person, Leena had barely reached till her ears and wore braces. And now here she was, a grown young doctor, with a smile that Mrs Gadkar found as beautiful as the sunrises she grew up watching over the rice farms in her village.

As Leena stared into space with the bowl forgotten in her lap, Mrs Gadkar reflected on how similar Leena's long straight nose was to her own late husband's. 'What are you thinking about, dear?' she asked.

Leena turned her head and sighed, 'Just thinking about the Masters exams. I took almost a year's break from work to study for them but they got cancelled. The clubs also got closed earlier so the bartending hobby I took up during this time stopped. And now we are locked in our houses.'

'I understand, *beta*.[3] But have faith. God does everything right in the end. You will score even better

---

[3] Child.

now and get admission in an even better university. And I am happy that the clubs are closed. What sort of a doctor does bartending anyway? Alcohol is bad for health, no?'

'Only *too much* alcohol is bad, *lah*. A little bit is okay. Mixing new drinks and serving them with flair is so much fun. I love the reactions I get from customers. I learnt so much at this professional bartending course. It would have helped me get a job at a reputed club and earn some money while studying in the US.'

'Students in the USA work at cafes to meet their living expenses. Why can't you also simply brew coffee?' asked Mrs Gadkar with narrowed eyes.

It was Leena's turn to scoff. 'Please, Aaji!' she protested and got distracted by a notification on her phone.

'Yes, yes. Just one pinch of turmeric is enough. Too much and it will become bitter.' Mrs Gadkar disconnected her Nokia phone with a pout and crossed out 28 April on the calendar.

She had become an overnight star among her son Shekhar's friends. Before his unexpected departure to London from Singapore, they had come over for dinner and she insisted on preparing the meal herself. Licking the *puran poli* and *saar*[4] off his fingers, Varun said, 'Maushi,[5] today I realised there is something that I miss even more than my mother back home. Her food!'

By the end of the evening, Mrs Gadkar's diary was full. During the twenty-five days of her stay in Singapore

---

[4] Jaggery stuffed flatbread and curry.
[5] Auntie, signifying a family feeling even though Mrs Gadkar is not Varun's aunt.

before the lockdown, she spent two to three afternoons every week teaching the way to make delicacies at one of those friends' houses. For the first time in sixty-seven years, people fought to stand beside her. They wrote down her instructions, laughed at her criticism of the city life thrust upon her after marriage, and complimented the patterns on her saris.

Mrs Gadkar recalled the complaints she used to make to her husband when she had become bold enough to call him out, 'Do your students cook food and wash dishes for you? No, right? *I* do that! After a full day at office, don't you think you should take me to the park in the evenings instead of conducting physics tuitions for university students?!' Tucking the sari *pallu*[6] at her waist, she forgave him silently and continued explaining the difference between *kala masala*[7] and *kalagoda masala*.

And now, just like Leena's exams, her lessons stopped abruptly. It occurred to her that there were so many hacks she had missed sharing with her pupils. The only hope for passing them on was if one of them called to clarify a recipe.

Mrs Gadkar carefully placed a lid on the various meals prepared for the day. She ran a finger over the dust-free tables and artefacts. She completed reading the last of the magazines kept in a cabinet beside the dining table. She switched off the TV that was running a soap episode she had watched twice.

---

[6] Loose end of sari hanging over the shoulder.

[7] Mixture of spices.

She made her way to Leena's room to see what she was up to and found her texting as usual. Rolling her eyes, she said, 'Leena give me your phone. I want to call my sister Prabha in India.'

'Aaji, please use the spare smartphone. You will learn how to use it quickly. If you could commute all alone in Singapore, what is a new phone?'

'Absolutely not. Prabha has one of these new kind of phones. She clicked something and lost half her pension savings. Five months later she is still making trips to the police station, and still using that phone! They are a curse, I tell you.'

'That happens only when you press something you are not supposed to. I am here. I will teach you what to do and what not to.'

'No, I still won't use it. I have my own Nokia which your grandfather had gifted me. I will use only that.'

'Use the smartphone only for some time while you are here *lah*. Later you use your own Nokia again.'

'No, I don't want to use the smartphone even for some time!'

'Then I also don't want to lend you my phone!'

Mrs Gadkar glared at Leena, and Leena scowled at the floor. Leena may have had her grandfather's nose, but her pout was just like her Aaji's. Muttering under the breath about lack of care for elders, Mrs Gadkar stormed out saying, 'Fine, I am going to NTUC to get groceries.'

'Aaji, wait!' exclaimed Leena.

'What happened?' asked Mrs Gadkar.

Leena clinked her glass with Mrs Gadkar's and said wickedly, 'Cheers!'

'Shameless girl. Don't you do dare treat my *solkadi*[8] like your alcohol.'

'Hahaha! Relax *lah*, Aaji. I am just pulling your leg.'

After taking a swig, Leena groaned, 'Can you believe we've been stuck at home for almost a month now? A month!'

'What's wrong with staying at home?'

'Umm, it's boring with nothing to do!'

'Your generation just doesn't like to stay at home. There are plenty of ways to stay entertained. Especially with all this technology. We didn't have all this in our village and still we managed.'

'I think it's unfair you had to move because of marriage even though you didn't really want to.'

'That's just how things were back then. Decisions were made for us. But times change. I could not speak up for myself but I could for Shekhar.'

'What do you mean?'

'Your granduncle, your grandfather's elder brother, was not happy when Shekhar moved here. He believed that children should always stay with and serve their parents and extended family.'

'Then?'

'I did not want to tie Shekhar down. And I trust him. He might change homes but he would never abandon his family.'

Leena contemplated how her own life might have been if she had grown up in India instead. Definitely no bartending for her there.

---

[8] An appetising drink made of coconut milk and kokum.

Mrs Gakdar said, 'Speaking of your granduncle, give me the phone. I want to make sure he is taking care of himself.'

Leena sighed, 'Aaji, you spend more time on my phone than I do. Use that other smartphone to make phone calls only. Don't do anything else.'

'I will press a button and something else will happen. Don't worry, I will speak only for some time.'

'I will dial the number for you on that other phone. You talk for however long you want.'

'Just give me your phone, stop being stubborn!'

Mrs Gadkar's nostalgia intensified with every step of her evening walk amid the sound of insects trilling in the grass along the pavement. The altered form of this slick foreign city was strangely reminiscent of the rustic village life of her girlhood. Clear skies, meditative routines, the buzz of silence and a soothing solitude.

The phone's ring brought Mrs Gadkar back to her role of a grandmother. She answered Leena's call and a pit formed in her stomach.

'What happened, *beta*? Why are you crying?'

Between sobs and sharp breaths, Leena said, 'My head is hurting. A lot.'

Mrs Gadkar's heart wrenched as she thought of Leena pulling her hair over a face distorted in pain, looking as if she would pass out at any moment. She was aware of the agony Leena went through when she had a migraine.

'Don't worry, *beta*. I am coming home right away. Take your medicine and don't cry. If you cry, it will hurt some more.'

'The medicine has finished. Can you get a Panadol when you come?'

'*Ho ki.*[9] I am very close to NTUC. Pan-aa-dol, right? I will be home in just a few minutes, *raja*.[10] Don't cry.'

Mrs Gadkar scurried towards NTUC but was stopped at the entrance by a man who looked like he had been in an argument. He asked her for an ID.

'ID? What is this happening? No one asked for one when I came a few days ago.'

'These are new rules now,' he said. You have to show your NRIC or driving license or some photo ID before you can go inside.'

'I am a tourist. I have a passport but it is at home. And my granddaughter is in a lot of pain. Can you please let me go in for now? I will get an ID next time.'

'No, no, no. Then you download an app now and scan your phone.'

'My phone is old, it cannot do things like that. And I just need some medicine for my granddaughter. She is having a very bad headache. Please let me go just for today.'

'No, no, no. You have to follow rules. You bring your ID or download the app.'

'But why don't you understand it's urgent?'

'Listen, there is a pandemic, okay? You must follow the rules.'

'Can't you just make one exception? I was not aware of these rules. I promise I will bring an ID next time onwards.'

---

[9] Yes, of course.
[10] Means 'king' but is also used as a fond term to address a child.

'Look, I have already been shouted at by my boss for something else. I am not going to risk anything again. You please show your ID or come back later.'

'Okay fine, fine. Then here is some money. Can you please go inside and get one Panadol for me?' Turning to the few people staring at her, Mrs Gadkar asked, 'Or can one of you please get it for me?'

'Maushi? What happened? Is there a problem?' asked Varun, emerging from behind Mrs Gadkar.

'Varun! *Beta*, can you please get one Panadol for me? Leena is having a migraine and there is no medicine in the house. And they are not letting me go inside without an ID.'

'Can't you download this app on your phone—'

'No, I can't! I don't have that sort of phone!'

'Okay, okay, don't worry. I will quickly go and get the tablets for you.'

Mrs Gadkar walked towards Leena who was sipping a glass of water on the sofa the next morning. 'Are you alright, my dear?' she asked, running her hand over Leena's head.

Leena looked at her with puffy eyes and said, 'Head is still heavy but it stopped aching. Sorry you got such a scare last night because of me.'

'*Arre*[11] no, *beta*. I am just glad you are not in pain anymore. I have made very simple and light *varan bhaat*.[12] Don't eat anything very heavy for some time. Or you can have *dahi bhaat*.[13] Whatever you like. Okay?'

---

[11] Has different meanings based on the context. Here it means 'hey'.

[12] Lentil soup and rice.

[13] Curd rice.

'Yes, Aaji. I will be fine now. What are you holding in your hand?'

Mrs Gadkar exhaled deeply and placed the spare smartphone on the teapoy. 'Whenever you feel fully alright, teach me how to use this phone.'

'Oh! How this sudden change of heart?'

'I never want to be so helpless that I can't take care of my own grandchildren.'

'Komal, if you crack anymore naughty jokes I will put you on mute,' said Mrs Gadkar.

'See, Komal, I told you only serious students are allowed here,' quipped Varun.

'Varun, I will put you also on mute if you keep blabbering nonsense.'

Leena chuckled as she watched Mrs Gadkar teaching her disciples who had increased from seven to fifteen. Mrs Gadkar winked at Leena and continued, 'I hope you enjoyed yourselves and learnt some new things. All of you also made the second month of this lockdown enjoyable for me. I am leaving tomorrow night but you can call me any time on WhatsApp or Zoom.'

Her students spoke up at once: 'We will keep troubling you, Maushi.' 'Maushi, thank you so much!' 'Maushi, you remind me just of my mother. Visit us again soon, Maushi.'

Mrs Gadkar ended the meeting and turned to Leena, who had a strange smile on her face.

'What?'

'Nothing. Your eyes become so pretty and shiny when you talk to your students.'

Mrs Gadkar blushed and was about to voice her dissent when Leena said, 'Aaji, can I ask you something?'

'Yes?'

'What is your name?'

Mrs Gadkar blinked in surprise. The last time she had acknowledged her own name was while filling the immigration form. 'It is Namrata.'

'See, I have taught you well. You will be able to take care of yourself even when you are on your own. Your father will be back in a few days, anyway. There are apples in the fridge. Eat something healthy between meals,' said Mrs Gadkar as she packed her belongings.

'Yees, Aajiiii,' drawled Leena.

And what else? Oh, I need to send a picture of the Vande Bharat[14] flight details to your uncle. I have to click this paperclip icon, right?'

'Absolutely right. I have also taught you well.'

Mrs Gadkar cupped Leena's cheek and said, 'Yes, you have. Now I can call you directly instead of relying on your uncle or father. You might just regret teaching this old woman how to use the phone when she calls you incessantly.'

'You should worry that *I* will be calling you all the time!'

'You are such a sweet child, *beta*. If only time hadn't passed so quickly.'

---

[14] Flights of the Vande Bharat Mission conducted by the Indian government to repatriate people stranded in other countries due to COVID-19 travel restrictions.

'I knooow! The lockdown is getting lifted in a few days. There are so many places I still want to show you. I also wanted to take you to the club once. That would have been fun.'

'Oh, that bartending again. *Beta*, please stop that. It is not good. People who go there are so unruly and spoilt. It is a risky business, this whole bartending thing.'

'That's what you said about smartphones also, Aaji. But used in the right way they are helpful, right? Of course there are risks in everything. But if you are careful, nothing will happen.'

Mrs Gadkar beamed with pride at her granddaughter's wisdom but was too proud to give in. 'I trust you are sensible enough to take care of yourself. But I still don't understand what you get out of mixing alcohol.'

'The same feeling that you get when you form the perfect *modak*.[15] You know how people have different personalities? Drinks also have a personality of their own. When someone asks me to recommend a cocktail, I look at that person—the clothes, mannerisms and the way they ask for a drink. I make something according to that and when they tell me they loved it, I feel … happy!'

Mrs Gadkar was amused. 'Is it? What sort of a drink would you make for me?'

Leena looked at her Aaji's neatly pleated white hair and blue sari. She always wore a gold chain and bangles which sounded her reassuring presence. She had the poise of a confident person unaware of her own strength.

Leena did not remember much about the time her mother had passed away. But she recalled crying quietly

---

[15] A sweet dumpling stuffed with coconut and jaggery.

into her Aaji's strong lap while Aaji's soft hands stroked her head. It occurred to Leena that she would not have been able to make it through the lockdown without her grandmother. Once again she had been there for her when Leena did not even know that she needed her.

'Hold on,' said Leena, and came back with two glasses and a bottle.

'What's this?'

'Wine. An elegant drink for a strong, elegant person,' she declared dramatically.

'Where did this come from? There is alcohol in this house?'

'Yup! This is from Baba's secret premium stash that he doesn't know I know about.'

'Shekhar drinks?!'

'Who did you think was the first person to teach me about alcohol?'

'Is this the thing to teach an only daughter? Has he no shame and culture? Just wait till Shekhar comes back!'

'Aaji ... look, he will scold me if he finds out that I told on him. Do you want me to get scolded?'

'I don't care. This is just not right.'

'Forget that, Aaji. Here, I am pouring a drink for both of us. To celebrate what we learnt together, and to cherish these last few hours before you leave. We don't know when we will meet again. Do you want to spend these last few moments angry?'

Mrs Gadkar looked sceptically at the wine. 'You want me to drink that?'

'Yes. A little bit is nothing. Baba will never find out. This will be our little secret.'

Leena handed one glass to Aaji and brought her own glass to her lips.

'Wait!' exclaimed Mrs Gadkar.

'What happened?' asked Leena.

'Cheers!'

Both of them giggled like girls. Leena extended her hand to clink the glass but Mrs Gadkar pushed it away in embarrassment. She sniffed at the liquid, took a tentative sip and looked sheepishly at Leena.

'And, Aaji?'

Mrs Gadkar tasted the wine that remained on her tongue and thought about 'home'. She had had to move out of her own home; her son chose to live in one away from her; she was locked down in that with her granddaughter. The bitterness gave way to a sweet aftertaste.

She switched on the smartphone that she was careful to put on flight mode before take-off. Plugging in her earphones, she mused at how she was scared to do this even with her old Nokia. As she leaned into the seat with closed eyes, her thoughts on the things she had grown to accept were accompanied by her favourite song. *Kuch sust kadam raste, kuch tez kadam raahein* …

11

Roses

Ilya Katrinnada Binte Zubaidi

After minutes of traversing narrow grid-like roads, the car came to a halt. Ayah[1] pulled the handbrakes and stepped out of the car. Elia and Ibu[2] followed suit, each of them holding onto a bottle of *air mawar*[3] in one hand and a plastic bag of assorted loose flowers in the other— *mawar*,[4] *melur*,[5] *cempaka*.[6]

'Oh no!'

'What happened?' Ayah asked.

'I didn't realise that the ground is muddy.' Elia looked down to find her slippers and tail end of her *jubah*[7] tinted in a gunk of brown.

'It rained last night. Watch where you're going. The concrete can be slippery,' Ibu chimed in. She led the way as Elia cautiously traced her steps.

'Assalamu'alaikum,[8] Elia muttered under her breath. Every one of her visits to the Pusara Abadi Muslim

---

[1] Dad.

[2] Mum.

[3] Rosewater.

[4] Rose.

[5] Jasmine.

[6] Magnolia.

[7] A loose, long-sleeved and ankle-length garment commonly worn by Muslim men and women.

[8] 'Peace be upon you', also a common greeting among Muslim communities.

Cemetery began with this greeting. She did not know if the inhabitants of the graves could hear her, but surely God did.

She had never been to this section of the cemetery before. Just like other parts of the cemetery, most of the graves here comprised concrete frames with a hollow rectangular centre filled with small stones. Headstones stood erect on one end of some graves, and both ends on others. She had learnt from Ibu's sister Cik Ya[9] that headstones wrapped in yellow cloth denoted a royal lineage of sorts, while those covered in white indicated otherwise. Elia wondered if the difference in colour mattered. Engraved on the sides of the graves' frames were the names of the deceased. It had become a habit of Elia's to read the name of every man and woman as she passed by their graves. *Maksalmina Bin Azani. Zalia Binte Muhammad. Rawi Bin Mahar. Norin Binte Abu Bakar.* She did not know why she did this, maybe as an act of courtesy while passing by. The dates of their deaths were stated below their names. Elia noticed that the graves here were only a few months old, which explained why their concrete frames looked crisp and new, void of stubborn overgrown weeds that otherwise found their way through the smallest of cracks.

'Here we are,' Ayah said as they gathered around a grave with a dark blue frame. *Sariah Binte Suradi telah kembali ke Rahmatullah pada Khamis, 21 Mei 2015,*[10] its inscription read. Colourful flower petals were nestled

---

[9] *Cik* refers to Auntie.

[10] Sariah Binte Suradi had returned to her Lord on Thursday, 21 May 2015.

amongst its grey stones. The sweet scent of rosewater filled the air around them. 'Seems like somebody came to visit in the morning.'

'Nenek[11] is well-loved by many,' Ibu remarked, her voice marked by a tinge of pride, peppered with an understandable longing for her mother.

Elia smiled to herself. It was true. She had only ever heard positive things about her late grandmother, even after she passed away. Every so often, Elia would discover a new detail about Nenek from her mother, aunt and extended relatives.

'You like these soda crackers? She loved to eat them with butter.'

'She was a busy old woman, you know! She always spent her days walking around Geylang with her friends.'

'Beautiful plate, eh? She bought it on my last shopping trip with her.'

Elia sometimes thought that God must have loved Nenek so much that she continued to live through those who loved her even as her body had been laid to rest.

Elia and her parents scattered loose flowers on Nenek's grave. Ibu and Ayah quietly uttered words of prayers. Elia was preoccupied with the petals on the stones, rearranging them to ensure an even distribution of red, white and yellow amidst a sea of grey, all the while thinking about Nenek: the relaxed way in which she dragged her feet when she walked, her big lips that were the envy of many and her wrinkled hand that she would never be able to hold again. A tear rolled down her left cheek as she uncapped a bottle of rosewater and

---

[11] Grandmother.

emptied it on the grave. Ibu gave her a second bottle and she did the same. The three of them then raised their cupped hands to their chests. Ayah led a brief supplication in Arabic, praying for God's Mercy, Blessings and Forgiveness upon Nenek.

'Amin… Amin … Amin … '[12] Elia and Ibu echoed. At the end of the supplication, they wiped their hands down their faces and got ready to leave. Elia looked down on Nenek's grave. She let her right hand rest on the headstone, allowing another tear to fall, this time landing on a rose petal. *See you on the other side.*

Walking back to the car, Elia saw clusters of people spread out around the cemetery. Daughters, sons, wives, husbands, grandchildren. Women clad in headscarves and full-length dresses; men dressed in long-sleeved shirts and long pants. Standing under the scorching midday sun, they were doing what Elia and her parents had done: adorning the graves with flowers, rosewater and supplications. About a decade ago, she had asked Ibu and Ayah about these customs. *Would it guarantee the deceased a spot in Heaven? Would it preserve their bodies that would otherwise decay in the soil underground?* her ten-year-old mind had wondered.

'This is their home on earth now,' Ayah replied.

'They can't maintain it on their own. We love them and they love us. So we remember them in our prayers, and help keep their homes clean, sweet-smelling and beautiful,' Ibu added.

---

[12] May God answer our prayers.

'1, 2, 3, smile!' The shutter on Cik Ya's camera clicked, and out came a Polaroid.

'Can I have a look?' Mateen grabbed the Polaroid from his mother's camera.

'Let me see!' Elia snatched the Polaroid from her cousin, the tight grip of her hands leaving fingerprints on it.

'Stop fighting. You're both no longer children. Do you want me to send you over to the *Cina buncit* next door?' Nenek joked. Elia and Martin chuckled. Twenty years ago, the mere mention of Nenek's non-existent neighbour would have caused both of them to cry out of fear. But they had since learnt that the Big-bellied Chinese Man was nothing but a myth of their grandmother's, conjured to discipline them when they were kids.

They both took a look at the Polaroid together. A cake in the foreground, a smiling Nenek and her two grandchildren in the middle ground, and Nenek's sea blue-painted wall in the background. Elia noticed that Nenek's smile was wider than usual. *Must be the Mothers' Day glow*, her heart whispered. After all, it was Nenek who had invited her two daughters, Ibu and Cik Ya, and grandchildren to her house for a celebration. She had also wanted them to collectively pray for Elia's upcoming two-month internship in Thailand which would span the month of Ramadan[13] and the beginning of Syawal.[14]

'Elia, stop looking at the photo. Time to cut the cake. Grab a knife, small plates and forks in the kitchen,' Ibu

---

[13] The ninth month of the Islamic calendar during which Muslims fast from dawn to dusk.

[14] The tenth month of the Islamic calendar during which Muslims celebrate the completion of the preceding fasting month.

ordered. Elia rolled her eyes. 'Don't be rude, young lady. It's a small cake, so make sure everyone gets enough.'

Elia dragged her feet to the kitchen, internally lamenting her fate. She did not understand why, between her and Mateen, *she* was always assigned to be the cake-cutter every time a celebration called for one. Even during larger gatherings involving her extended family, *she* would be the one tasked to carry out this role as her five other male second cousins waited for their share of the cake. *Tsk, if boys don't know how to cut cake, then they don't deserve to eat it!* she muttered to herself as she opened Nenek's kitchen drawer.

'Elia, why are you taking so long?' Cik Ya called from the living room.

Elia took out a set of cream-coloured plates embellished with red floral brushstrokes and rushed back to the living room. Nenek smiled when she saw the plates in Elia's hands.

'That's my favourite set. Mrs Jones gave it to me,' she said.

Like other women during her time, Nenek got married at the young age of nineteen. The marriage was short-lived. Her husband had fallen for a woman he met while working his rounds as a postman. He was rightly aware that Nenek would not agree to him having a second wife, so the solemnisation happened up north across the Causeway[15] without her knowledge. Over a year, his

---

[15] The Johor–Singapore Causeway, a 1,056-metre causeway that links the city of Johor Bahru in Malaysia across the Straits of Johor to the town of Woodlands in Singapore.

financial provisions to Nenek and two-year-old Ibu, as his physical presence, steadily dwindled. Nenek's growing suspicion was confirmed when she stumbled upon his marriage certificate while cleaning the house. She fought to sign the divorce papers as soon as possible, all the while carrying Cik Ya in her belly.

Nenek knew she could no longer rely on her ex-husband for their survival even though he was legally obligated to monetarily support his children. She moved back in with her parents, taking up several odd jobs to contribute to the household income. In the meantime, word about her divorce had spread around their extended family and village. People, in particular women, looked at her with disdain in their eyes. *Unfaithful. Irresponsible. Selfish.* Nenek had these words, and more, thrown at her behind her back. Yet she continued turning up for communal gatherings on weekends with a silent, calm smile on her face.

Soon Nenek found a stable job—and unexpected joy—in the Jones' family home. Every weekday morning, she would turn up at their doorstep in Bukit Timah and spend the day cleaning their two-storey terrace house, sweeping, mopping, wiping the furniture, for a start. Her favourite chore was ensuring that their display cabinets of exquisite tableware was free of dust and dirt. Mr and Mrs Jones, expats from the other side of the globe, enjoyed buying plates, cups and utensils on their travels. They had amassed an impressive collection. Every time she wiped them clean, Nenek would also take the opportunity to admire the thoughtful designs—blue-glazed bowls from China, serving platters decorated with basket-inspired dotted concentric circles from

Zimbabwe, coasters in the shape of banana leaves from Indonesia.

Nenek earned the praise of her employers, who entrusted her with the keys to their house six months into the job. She was quick to earn pay raise after pay raise throughout her twenty years of service. Not only was the money enough to cover her ailing parents' medical fees, she could afford to send her two daughters to school all the way till post-secondary level, a first in the history of her family. She always had extra cash to donate, and to help her backbiting relatives who faced financial stress. When the Joneses left Singapore to move back to their hometown, they gifted her with her favourite set of rose-inspired dessert plates, which she kept in her kitchen drawer for her granddaughter to find twenty years later.

'How's the cake? *Sedap*?'[16] Ibu asked. Both Elia and Mateen nodded their heads simultaneously. Down to their last bite, they were savouring every bit of the strawberry shortcake left on each of their plates.

'Nenek, this cake is so *sedap*. Can you bake this for me when I come back from Thailand?' Elia asked. Nenek kept mum. She was more well-versed in making Malay *kuih*.[17] Realising this, Elia cheekily added, 'Actually, why don't you make me my favourite pineapple tarts instead?'

'Without the pineapple topping?'

'Of course! You know me well, Nenek.' Elia licked her lips upon finishing her last bite of the cake.

---

[16] Delicious.

[17] An umbrella term for bite-sized snacks or desserts commonly served in Southeast Asia that typically come in the form of cakes, cookies, dumplings, pudding, biscuits and pastries.

'Elia, bring the plates and forks back to the kitchen. Clear the cake box. Make sure you wash them,' Ibu ordered. Elia rolled her eyes again at being chosen to clear the plates.

'It's okay, Elia. Just leave them in the sink.'

'No, Nenek, I'll do the dishes so you can rest tonight!' Elia exclaimed. Nenek smiled and gave her a nod of thanks.

While washing the dishes, Elia pumped extra liquid soap onto the sponge to get rid of any residual whipped cream. After wiping them dry, she gently placed them one by one in the drawer, taking the time to observe the flowers on the them. *The plates are decades old. And the roses are still in bloom. Just like my grandmother.*

III

Precarity and Tenacity

12

November Hope

Rolinda Onates Española

The first time I came to Singapore, I stayed for twelve days at the agency's accommodation. It was one of the hardest times I had living abroad. The accommodation was in a very big building; my agency was one of the biggest maid agencies in Singapore. The rooms were full of bunkbeds with no pillows and blankets. Maids were categorised by their nationality. In that building there were Burmese girls, very young ones, while it seems that others had just hit puberty. The Indonesians seemed like tough ladies. The Chinese also could be seen and, of course, we Filipinas, the friendly ones. The nights were cold as in November there are heavy rains. We covered ourselves in hope that we wished would lead us to sleep each night, praying in the morning that our names would be called for pick up.

I imagined myself incarcerated in a women's detention cell. But what was my case? Was it a crime to dream of a better life? Not so much for me but more so for my family. The agents briefed us on what we needed to do. Our luggage was in a locker room outside the building. We just needed to get two sets of clothes and underwear, and put it in a plastic bag, that is, if you had one. If didn't then you'd need to carry your personal things with you as the lock room was only open at a specific hour in the morning. Everybody needed to shower first thing in the day. Then we would go down to the basement where the food was served. Our food was rationed and was usually an omelette with flour and sauteed cabbage. I hadn't known about this recipe before but, I assure you, you wouldn't end up wishing for more. For twelve days I never had meat in my meal, yet at that time, another hope helped us swallow it down.

I had pocket money of 1,500 Filipino pesos in my wallet. Since I'm a coffee person I traded 500 for ten sachets of Nescafé and one packet of biscuits. The agents at the office had a small business of much too much expensive items but I had no choice. I was planning to make it last until my employer fetched me, though I should have been saving money. In the mornings I couldn't drink alone with others staring at me. Anyway, my biscuits disappeared and went into someone else's mouth while I was in the shower. 'Sharing' can result in them letting you sip your coffee peacefully though you miss your biscuits to dip into it just like hope.

I never learned sympathy in that place. I learned empathy, I learned to listen even if I didn't understand the words. I learned to care more universally. I learned to feel how vulnerable and invaluable we were as maids. I learned that if you could communicate better, they would give you extra tasks and if you couldn't speak English properly everyone would bully you, even your own countrymen. But then, we embraced hope. Faith in hope was always our guiding light.

The morning my name was announced for pick up, I promised myself to never go back to that place, never again—even if it was a strange sort of non-home to me for a time.

My hope never failed me, and yet I wonder what happened to the others. Did they tell their stories too? Did they have the courage to do so? Until now, I keep wondering about them.

13

Knock Knock! Who's There?

Work from Home Stranger

Anjali Patil

It was the messiest I had seen the living room since I came to work for Ma'am and Sir, more than a year ago. Three large computer screens, two laptops, a keyboard, a mouse, extension cords and a bulky pile of wires of different types were all stacked up in one corner of the living room that I worked very hard to keep like homes in lifestyle magazines. Just the way Ma'am liked it. Now, one corner of that picture-perfect living room looked like the shabby storeroom of an electronics store.

Usually, when they were going to buy something, Ma'am and Sir told me in advance where to make space for it. That Friday evening when I opened the door, I was surprised and could not understand where they had got all these things from. They weren't packed in boxes; they didn't look new. Trying to figure out where all of it would fit in was making me crazy.

'Did you hear the news, Melina?' Ma'am asked. 'Singapore is going into a lockdown. Remember I told you how everything has been closed in India? It's going to be shut here, too, for one month. So Ajai and I will work from home.'

I only half-heard that, my mind still on the messy corner.

'Where will we put all of this, Ma'am?'

I did not say it, but there was no space in the small apartment.

'Ajai and I will rearrange some things tomorrow morning. We have the weekend to set it up.'

And that is how the dinner table became Ma'am and Sir's office. Only half of it, though. Ma'am insisted that the other half would remain clear to dine on as she was very particular about eating their only meal together at the table. Every evening, they talked about their day and laughed at stories about each other's colleagues, whom each knew only by name, or nicknames that the other gave them—Miss Perfectionist consultant, Forever-on-a-diet copywriter, Yes-man client services director and other less complimentary ones.

The next morning, while Sir was setting up the computers on one half of the table, Ma'am and I were folding the tablecloth to cover the other half, which had on it a pitcher of lemon water, a fruit bowl and some glasses. The set-up looked odd. Big computer screens—one on Sir's side and two on Ma'am's side—crowded the tabletop. The unending wires connecting the various devices criss-crossed the table and the longer ones ran down the sides to the extension cords on the floor. The clutter was awful. The dining side of the table looked overrun and out of place.

'Vini, can we not use the full table?' Ajai asked. 'This is too cramped. There's no place for our mobile phones, tablets, scribble pads, stationery …'

Ma'am found a way and, minutes later, it was all stacked up on two antique teapoys that we moved from near the sofa and placed on either side of the dinner table. She would not budge on the subject of eating dinner at the table. I wondered what they would talk about. Seated across from each other for the full day, they would know exactly how it had been. And there were no weekends or vacations to plan.

In the first week, there was much excitement about working from home. Everything went without a hitch, they took coffee and lunch breaks together and did not seem to miss their office routine. Late evenings, they would go for a walk to Fort Canning or to the supermarket on Killiney Road or pick up a takeaway dinner from Robertson Quay. They were together all the time and seemed to be enjoying it.

'That was not so bad. Week one down,' Vini said.

'Quite fun, actually. I could get used to it,' Ajai replied.

'I don't know why we said that we would never work together. Maybe we could be colleagues in the future.'

I saw different sides of Ma'am and Sir. They were so boss-like when speaking on the phone. It was quite different from the way they spoke to me. They sounded matter of fact while telling their teams what to do and when to get it ready by. Sometimes I heard anger in their voices when things were not done to their liking. At times they would sit up straight. Speaking to their boss, I imagined. Sometimes, they would comment on what they had heard the other say.

'Vini, you were too harsh on that poor bloke.'

'It's consulting, not advertising, Ajai. You are too nice to your team.'

I could hear only one side of the conversation because they used earphones, not that I tried to eavesdrop. The apartment was small and whether I was cleaning the bedroom or cooking, their voices could be heard loud and clear. As the days passed, I tuned them out because I could not understand what they talked about.

But on Tuesday afternoon in the second week, Sir was checking his e-mail, Ma'am was on the phone and I was in the kitchen. I was not really listening until suddenly I heard a change in Ma'am's tone. It was a work call but she sounded casual, chatty almost. Like you would chat with a boyfriend. Her voice sounded louder as Sir stopped typing. He was staring at his screen, but I knew he was listening.

'Miss seeing you, too,' Vini said and took off her earphones. She had a half-smile, the kind when things turn out as you want them to.

'Who was that?' Ajai asked. He spoke softly, but I heard the note of displeasure in his voice. Ma'am, it would seem, didn't.

'Nick. He's a new partner in accounting. Moved here from Dublin a few months ago. I'm working with him on a project for one of my consulting clients.'

'Why were you flirting with him?'

In the one year that I had worked for them, I had never seen them get into a fight. Small arguments at times, but never a fight. This seemed like the beginning of one.

'That was flirting? What are you getting at, Ajai? I've heard you punctuate every other request with "be a sweetheart" these past few days. I didn't ask you about that.'

'You should have. I would have told you. Doesn't mean a thing.'

'And I told you. It was Nick. I need his help with a project and was trying to build a rapport with him. Completely harmless.'

'It sounded like flirting and I didn't like it.'

'Grow up, Ajai. It meant nothing.'

I turned off the gas stove and went to my room. I feel uncomfortable witnessing a fight. They continued talking, their voices raised, but I couldn't hear what they were saying. After a while, Ma'am went out for a walk alone and returned a couple of hours later. Dinner was quick and quiet that day.

I think Sir was right, I said to my husband when I called him that night. He agreed. I knew that he would, and it was one of the reasons why I said it. I did not want to start an argument between us by saying that Ma'am was not wrong either. The other reason was that, after watching them for a year, I had come to the conclusion that Sir loved Ma'am more than she loved him. I don't think he doubted her. He was jealous. I was sure that if they worked from home for long, their relationship would suffer.

I wanted to tell them to be grateful for how lucky they were. They were together, they could continue working even during the circuit breaker and got to keep their jobs. I did not have the choice of working from home. Other people's homes were my workplace. Even here in Singapore, with Ma'am and Sir, I had made a home but it was not my home. I wished I could go back to my family whom I hadn't seen for more than a year. But I couldn't. I was the only one earning an income now. My husband, who ferried tourists in his taxi back home in Darjeeling, was grounded in the lockdown. And it was going to be a long time before the tourists returned.

The next room that their work invaded was the bedroom, the only other room in the apartment, besides the kitchen and the living room. There was my windowless matchbox room, but Ma'am only ever stepped in for the occasional surprise check. After the argument over Nick they would take their calls turn by turn from the bedroom, closing the door behind them. It was an unspoken agreement. Their home had easily become their workspace. But bringing home who they were at work was creating problems. That shut door marked a boundary beyond which they could put on their work masks for their colleagues. And with Zoom calls increasing, they spent more and more time in separate rooms and told each other stories, as they used to when they worked from the office.

'Vini, we haven't had dinner at the table for a couple of weeks. Could we not use the full table for work? It's really difficult to manage with only half,' Ajai grumbled.

That evening, Ma'am asked me to put away the tablecloth. Within three weeks of working from home enough had changed for her to let go, without a whisper of an argument, her insistence on having dinner at the table.

When they were together, in front of their laptops or at lunch and dinner, they were both careful to avoid topics that would set off an argument. It got harder with each passing day of the circuit breaker, when they saw no one but each other—and me.

One early afternoon Ajai said, 'We've got an informal team call coming up in two weeks to talk about something new that we learnt during the circuit breaker, the lessons it taught us. Any ideas?'

'Huh? None,' Vini answered without looking up from her laptop.

'I plan to say baking.'

'Yeah. Sure. Why not? Or yoga.'

'The call's in two weeks. I can't learn yoga by then.'

'And you can learn baking? You've never stepped foot into the kitchen.'

'When was the last time *you* saw the kitchen?' Ajai asked. 'If you ever have to talk about what you learnt during the circuit breaker, here's a sure-fire one for you— you learnt to be nasty!'

I no longer reacted to these word bombs, as I called them. They dropped every now and then, leading to arguments. A cold silence would follow, lasting days, and when they seemed to be putting it behind them, another word bomb would drop. The only time I worried was if my name came up. Because then, whatever the problem, it could become my fault and I would be blamed. There was no one else.

Ma'am did not reply to the 'nasty' remark. The afternoon wore on in complete silence and when I retired to my room, the only sounds were those of the clicks of their keyboards and the pings of WhatsApp messages. It was a tense silence. Or maybe I was anxious. But worse was to come. The words already exchanged were not the most hurtful they said to each other that day. It was the day the circuit breaker was extended until June.

Around three o'clock, the silence of the afternoon was broken by their ringing phones and excited conversations about a press conference and what might be announced. At four o'clock, they switched on the television. When the circuit breaker extension was announced, we were dazed.

'Did they just say another five weeks?' Ajai asked.

'Damn! I can't do this anymore,' Vini exclaimed.

'Hey, hey, it's not like we have a choice.' He put his arm around her, but she pulled away. 'Wait. What can't you do anymore?' he asked.

'This. Be with you all the time.'

Sir seemed to be stunned into silence.

'It's a lifetime of "this" we committed to,' he said finally. 'Hasn't been that long since you said you couldn't live without me, that we should never be apart.'

Another silence, longer this time.

'It was never 24x7, right? No one ever meant it this way. With no break from each other. At all,' Vini said.

'You think it's easy for me?'

Oh no, no, no. This was getting ugly. I wanted to go to my room and stay there until it was over. But I had been cleaning the bedroom and would have to pass by them to go to my room. Better to hide where I was. Neither of them spoke. After many minutes passed, I peeped out to see if they had gone back to working but they were just sitting on the sofa, staring at each other. They looked broken-hearted, wondering cluelessly about what had got them to this point. Then their phones rang and computers beeped, and they put on their earphones and continued working late in the evening. There was no storming out of the house. There was nowhere to go. And no one to go to.

Ma'am and Sir had a strange way of dealing with their problems. They would say something hurtful and then retreat, not wanting to cause each other more pain but not letting their love show either. I couldn't bear to see them like this. I felt like telling them that it is best to not carry a fight into the next day. We had that pact—my husband and I. Back home, when we were together, we fought bitterly over silly things. Even now, when we were stuck in different countries and did not know when we would meet again and spoke to each other only once a day, we would sometimes get into an argument. But we would always text each other and make up before calling it a night.

Their routine changed a great deal in the weeks that followed. Ma'am and Sir tried to spend as little time together as possible. They worked without a break, eating lunch mindlessly. As the number of conference calls increased, they were in different rooms for hours at a time. Ma'am took to running in the evenings. She would finish work and go for a long run, returning just in time for dinner. They still ate together but in front of the television, sometimes watching Netflix well into the night. That made it easier to not say anything to each other. When they talked, they spoke about everything and everyone but themselves. There was no one for whom they had to keep up appearances, or hide that they were living more separate lives than in the past, except on Zoom calls with family and friends. But pretending for an hour is not difficult, is it?

One evening Ma'am came home from her run, completely drenched by the sudden, heavy rain. Even after a hot shower, she was shivering. Sir fussed over her. I made her some of her favourite *laksa* noodle soup.[1]

By the next morning, she had fever and was sneezing. They went to the doctor and I was concerned as they were not back even at noon. When they got home, they both looked very worried. The doctor had asked for a COVID test as a precaution. I gave them some masala chai,[2] even while thundery rain continued to come down hard, as it sometimes does in Singapore. They sat together, lost in thought, no doubt imagining the worst. Both needed comforting but they remained silent. And when Ma'am spoke, I wished, for once, that the silence had remained unbroken.

'If I test positive, you'll have the house to yourself for a few weeks. Maybe even longer.'

'That's a terrible thing to say.'

It was. I heard the pain in Sir's voice. I think that Ma'am too knew that Sir loved her more than she loved him. Every once in a way, she would speak about something terrible happening to her, just to hear Sir express his concern and tell her how much he loved her.

'You really think that having the house to myself matters more than you? Do you really believe that?' Ajai asked.

---

[1] *Laksa* is a spicy noodle soup popular in the Peranakan cuisine of Southeast Asia. It consists of thick wheat noodles or rice vermicelli with chicken, prawn or fish, served in spicy soup based on either rich and spicy curry coconut milk or on sour *asam* (tamarind).

[2] Masala chai is a tea beverage made by boiling black tea in milk and water with a mixture of aromatic herbs and spices.

'You said that it's not easy for you to be around me.'

Ah, finally they were going to deal with *that* abandoned conversation.

'I said it's not easy being around you all the time. You said you couldn't do it 24x7 either. I was disturbed by that fight we had and afraid of losing you. We weren't talking and I didn't know what to do. So, I called the Samaritans helpline. The counsellor explained that we become different people at work. When we brought our work avatars into our home, we met these strangers for the first time. We didn't give ourselves a chance to get to know them. And then we tried hiding them from each other—going into a different room when we had to let them out among the people who know them.'

Sir explained it so well. He is very good at saying things with nice words in a nice way. I wouldn't have been able to although I knew what the problem was. But then, who was I to tell them whom to bring into their home?

How was it that I figured out the problem? Because the person I am in their home—my workplace—is very different from who I really am. Here, I speak softly. I don't voice my opinions unless I'm asked. If I want to disagree, I try and find a proper time and way of saying it. But that's not someone my husband will recognise. He will laugh if Sir or Ma'am compliment me for being like this. He will say that you are talking about a stranger. You should see her at home in Darjeeling. She is like a tigress. He is right. But then, that is a story for another day.

Back to Sir and Ma'am. After a tense day of waiting, the test result was negative. They celebrated, laughed and talked as they hadn't in weeks.

From then on, whenever their phones rang and they had to put on their work avatars, they would make the peace sign to ask for understanding for their temporary work selves. It never stopped being comical to me, but it kept the peace alright and brought back the loving couple I knew.

14

Maid in Singapore

Audrey Tay

Young Man to Traveller: Where is your home?

Traveller to Young Man: Home is where the heart is no longer shackled to the imprisoning norms and prejudices—self-imposed and otherwise—that bind it, so that it is now free to soar and seek the paths that lead it home, to recover a forgotten but still familiar haven that releases its perfume of security, comfort and finality of destination, encircling the man so that he no longer welcomes the need to leave.

The dog and I walk down the garden path in the early evening light, or rather he strains on the leash and pulls. Ahead is his friend, the Pomeranian Mica from the fourth floor. I, on the other hand, am plodding along, my too-big slippers going 'flup-flup'. I am determined that, in this moment, free from the confines of home, no one, least of all an animal, should dictate my pace.

It is a losing battle. The dog has the powerful muscle strength of his Jack Russell breed that I cannot match. I let myself be dragged along.

The two dogs circle each other politely, nose to butt. It is as if they have just met, even though they have known each other from four years ago when one (Mica) was one and the other seven months old. They do not gambol together, nip at each other in play like my village dogs do. Mica's new Myanmar helper cannot speak English, so we smile, our greeting as courteous as the dogs'. My English is passable: three years in Singapore has ensured that. I miss Dewi, the previous helper who was recalled home for good three weeks ago to get married to a man of her family's choosing, someone she does not know. Her village in Sulawesi is three hours away from mine. Nonetheless, I gave her my previous month's wages of $650 for my big brother Budi, to save on bank-transfer fees. Budi will borrow a motorbike to get the money.

I wonder how he is doing. During our last conversation two weeks ago, Budi talked about the dwindling fish stocks even as the weather has been clement. He mentioned that the well pump needed repairing. Until it was restored to working order, each household had to buy water from the village head at a premium to compensate him for his efforts in procuring the precious resource from the next village. I lapped up the news, my hunger making me greedy, and pressed Budi for the smallest details.

Even the bad news about the pump could not dampen Budi's excitement, for his wife is due to give birth to their first child any time. The village midwife is on standby; no one is taking chances, especially after two miscarriages. The couple pray for a boy; I just want the baby to be healthy, whatever its gender.

The Internet connection in our village is patchy at best and our messages sometimes arrive all at once, weeks late. Maybe the next time I hear from Budi and his wife, they would be a family of three. I cannot wait for the happy news, even if the information is tardy.

They are living in the house left us by our deceased parents. It is not much, just a corrugated tin roof supported by misaligned wooden slats that do nothing to keep out the rain, wind, insects and neighbours. The house needs constant repair, and I am amazed that it is still standing. It must be due to my brother's exemplary handyman's skills. But it is not passed on between siblings because each time anything breaks down here, Old Mistress calls me useless and rings for a professional.

Budi and I want our new brick house to be filled with ever-constant laughter and to be a solace for his future children. We will put in modern conveniences where running water would flow at the turn of a tap. No longer would anyone need to leave the house to use a lavatory dug in the ground. We women would be grateful, especially during that time of the month. We would say: let there be light and so it would be so with the flip of a switch. Goodbye to smelly kerosene and fire hazards. And no more mad scrambles to assemble pails to catch the thick ropes of rain streaming through the holes.

Only the foundation of the house has been laid so far. It is a start. In another five years, I reckon we would be able to add three storeys. It has been agreed that I will have the top floor to myself and Budi and his family will live on the lower floors. I don't mind the climb and maybe if we build high enough, I can see the sea.

I yearn for it so much.

The waves, they nurture me. My mother used to worry whenever she spotted me standing alone in the water, but she need not have because I am among friends. My entire body moves of its own volition in sync with the furious dance of the wild, rising waves, their frothy spray enfolding and engulfing me. They hold me tight in their embrace, our oneness comforts me. I can forget, I am forgotten, I am accepted, I am released. And the waves whisper their stories of adventures in lands beyond the horizon, borne along on the wings of winds. They speak of places they have been where buildings stretch up to touch the feet of God, dressed in twinkling red, blue, yellow, all the colours of the rainbow that glow bright in the night and whose streets glitter litter-free in the sunlight. Where you will earn in six months what you cannot even get in as many years in the village.

No one understands these dreams, not even my family. I don't explain anymore.

Parco the dog has had enough of excitement and wants to go home. Home is that tiny flat we share with Old Mistress, a rectangular box at the intersection of a certain row and column in a ubiquitous block of similarly styled flats. We disappear into the bowels of our box on the twenty-sixth floor, anonymous to the outside world as soon as the door closes behind us.

Old Mistress is hungry, but her dinner (and thus mine) is easy to prepare: fish and rice porridge and an assortment of vegetables. No salt or monosodium glutamate as I have to be mindful of her high blood pressure and allergies. This food of the rich takes some getting used to. It is strange because no aroma breaks free to entice the empty stomach.

Back in the village, we seldom eat meat or the good fish. We may be a fishing village but whatever daily catch the men haul in is destined for sale. The expensive fish sells out quickly, but the unwanted fish then becomes the family meal. We buy broken rice and the straggly vegetables our barren sands offer, and pair these with homemade fish sauce. Each family has its own recipe. When every household settles down for the evening meal, a collective flavour is released. It rises to float and mingle with the salty air, a sultry mistress beckoning the hungry to partake of her sweetness. That smell is our dinner bell.

Two years to the day after they found my father's body washed ashore after his boat capsized, and four months after we lowered my mother into the ground (the doctor said it was a ruptured appendix, but we know it was a broken heart), I announced to Budi that I was going to Singapore.

'What? Where? Why do you want to leave? This ...' here Budi flapped his arms, 'is your home. You have everything here. I am twenty years old and strong; I can support you. As it is, I catch almost as much *Rappo-Rappo*[1] as Pak Azam!'

'Bung (older brother), even Pak Azam the wonder fisherman can barely feed his family. I will earn enough to have us feast on *udang laut besar*[2] every day and still have enough left over to build us a palace.'

'*Udang laut* ... palace ...' Budi gaped, slack-jawed, a prominent vein throbbing in his left temple. 'What sacrilegious talk is this? It's all that sea worship you do that has hurt your head and caused such unbelievable nonsense to sprout from your heart. No one leaves home, even if it is not perfect. Here is our lifegiving mother and father. We are born here, and we will die here. Even

[1] Yellowtail fusilier.
[2] Big prawns.

if starvation or disease takes us, we will lie in this very soil that has birthed and suckled our forefathers. It is the proper way. It has been so for generations and it will be so for many more. Who put these radical ideas into your head? Don't give me that poppycock about the sea calling to you!' Budi shouted.

'I am a man now and the head of this family. So, you, Nela, would do well to listen to me! It is time to find you a husband. Stop saying that you want to find your own. Our elders decide these things because the years have given them wisdom. Mama was only sixteen when she got married. You are now nineteen, so you have been spoiled enough. With a husband and children, you will never again think of abandoning this life, you will never turn your back on your very own home!'

I left in the dead of the night. Only the village dogs saw me off.

After Old Mistress' dinner, I take mine with Parco for company. He wolfs down his premium air-dried beef, a handful of organic blueberries and a half apple. Parco's food is very expensive, especially the blueberries which I myself have never tasted. Old Mistress says she does not spare any expense when it concerns her 'son'.

I slice the other half of the apple for Old Mistress. She sits in front of the TV, apple to mouth, while her eyes remain fixated on the Korean drama with its screaming and scheming *ajumma*s[3] hell-bent on separating the star-crossed young lovers. I sit at her feet to massage them while keeping my head low to avoid blocking her view. Old Mistress grunts and shifts. I have learnt to change

---

[3] Married, or middle-aged, women.

the pressure and position applied according to the pitch and intensity of the grunts.

Only after Old Mistress has gone to bed do I and Parco retire to our room. Technically Parco has his own bedroom, next to Old Mistress'. But Parco took a shine to me soon after I started working for Old Mistress and insists on sleeping next to me. His mattress is well-padded and twice as large as his body so that when he tosses and turns, he does not end up on the cold, hard floor. We have moved it next to mine.

My mattress too lies on the floor. It fits the exact dimensions of my room, leaving little wriggle leeway. I have been conditioned from a young age to not move too much in my sleep, sandwiched as I was between Budi and our mother while our father slept outdoors. So, the space (or lack thereof) does not bother me much. Above my mattress, shelves are lined one on top of the other on two sides of the walls, going all the way to the ceiling. Old Mistress gave me one wall for my things, and the other is for cleaning products and spare towels. It makes sense because my room is in the kitchen and I don't have to run too far to get supplies. I cannot close the door fully, though, and so Parco and I sleep like this, one on each side of the open door, heads almost touching.

Old Mistress hardly steps into my domain. She has an en-suite toilet in the master bedroom and spends her days shuffling from this bedroom to the living room and then back to her room. Once, she went to Parco's old room (now empty) and wondered out loud if she should rent it out, offering cleaning services and catered meals with it to get a higher income. I knew better than to volunteer my opinion and was relieved when the matter was eventually shelved.

I am lucky to have gotten Old Mistress. She does not beat me. She does not burn me with hot pans when angry. She screams at me and jabs my forehead with an index finger when she thinks I am slow in executing her orders but then she forgets the unhappiness quickly. Sometimes, during the foot massage (and commercial break), she pats my head and say, 'Nela, you are *almost* like the daughter I never had, if only you had been born here. I might even have been tempted to adopt you for you know I have no family but Parco. But you are merely a stupid maid. You do serve me well enough, though, and I have not yet caught you stealing. I am also not worried you will fall pregnant because which man will fall for your fat and square body? That is why I picked you. Anyway, you must remain with me until I die. I will not allow you a transfer to another employer. Changing maids is *such* a hassle and those maid agencies are bloodsuckers. Imagine charging exorbitant fees just to press a few computer buttons.'

The thing I am most grateful to Old Mistress for is my room. My sanity preserver. Many of my friends have to sleep in their charges' rooms (children or bedridden elderly) and do not get sufficient sleep, let alone privacy. I know my friends typically get up at 5 am to make breakfast for the school-going children of the family before tending to the elderly members and the chores. They do not stop working until past 11 pm or later when the family goes to bed. What is left over for down time?

Old Mistress does not need me from 10 pm to 7 am. On the rare occasion that she does, she rings a bell in the middle of the night for a leg massage. The swelling

163

causes pain that neither medication nor massages can relieve but Old Mistress is comforted by my presence. However, once I am in my room, I am the sole mistress of this space—mine to command and do as I will. This is where I have plastered the only photo of my parents and Budi and his wife on their wedding day on the one shelf-less wall. Over the three years I have lived here it has faded somewhat, but I have added enough of my own photos (taken solo or with friends on our days off) to form a colourful montage. This is what lulls me to sleep, a nightly reminder that even as I am alone, I am not.

Tonight, as I lie in the semi-darkness, with light from the opposite building filtering in through the curtain-less kitchen window and Parco snoring gently, I remember the outing on my day off two Sundays ago. It was my birthday and, as it had been for the past three years, I had chosen to spend it by myself, at the beach. There were no crashing waves. Even in a thunderstorm the waves do not get angry, contrary to the people here who get mad and impatient easily. Drivers do not wait for you to cross safely to the other side before they start inching their cars onto your path. Hawkers shout at you if you are slow in ordering your food. MRT passengers push past you the moment the train doors open. In my early days I would cry, certain that I would never be able to survive this relentless animosity. At other times, when I am not perceived as an irritant, I remain a nonentity to the vast majority, just another faceless statistic in a regulated community of 250,000 Foreign Domestic Workers (our official job title), never welcomed but marginally tolerated.

However, my perception has since changed, and I no longer mind so much. Because I understand the people better. They have to work hard to earn the cash to buy their million-dollar condos (or get them on credit), spend days golfing at the country club and chauffeur their children (or dogs, in Old Mistress' case) in their expensive cars to enrichment classes (Parco has twice-weekly sessions of swim play). Old Mistress revealed this to me the day I accidentally left a tiny scratch on her car while washing it.

'You brainless, clumsy thing! Do you think that this car is cheap enough for you to damage? It costs $100,000 mind you. Do you even know how much that is? You will never see that kind of money in your lifetime, not even two!' *Pootui.* Old Mistress' spittle landed at my feet, fortuitously off the mark.

'So, I now have to get it repaired. You think my money just rains down from the sky? I had to work hard for it, to pay for everything: the car, the condo, the club and even you!' Old Mistress paused long enough to administer a stinging slap. 'I am docking one month's pay from you!'

All this chasing after money must be wearisome and although many do not attain success, they do not stop trying. That is why they are stingy with their kindness: their hearts are too weighed down by an endless burden to be open and generous.

Like the people here, I too am pursuing my dream. I wish for the good health to continue working towards building my own house and contribute to my family's happiness. In my case, my dream will be realised. Time is the key to its success. Another five years. Five short years yet five long years.

That day at the beach, I asked the waves what home would be like at the end of this waiting period. Would it be the old one I had left three years ago, untouched by the passage of time through which I could slip into as if I had never gone? Or would it be an old-new one, comforting in its familiarity of recalled memories but different enough to tell me that I no longer quite belong? Or a mix of both or of nothing, that, in fact, I am the changed one and that it would be up to me to drop my anchor in the safe harbour of my choosing?

And, as always, the waves that see everything, even the hearts of men, sang me their never-changing lullaby. I nodded, for I knew they would transport me home, come what may.

15

The Pangolin

Euginia Tan

The man caught sight of the departing bus from the staircase landing. He rushed awkwardly down the stairs, the extra fold of his stomach flopping out like a loose tongue. His dress shoes landed too hard on the concrete pavement, the arch of his feet briefly seared with a piercing pain. He feebly flagged the bus from a distance behind as it began to move away, letting out a hiss like the opening of a soft-drink can. It was the third bus that week he had missed. He lumbered to the bus-stop seats, covering his distended belly with his office bag as he sat down to wait for the next one.

Perspiration pooled at the nose bridge of his spectacles. He pushed them up with his left arm, catching a whiff of sour-armpit stench. The spectacles propped up for a minute, then slid down again. He left them at the brink of his nose, allowing the night to smudge around him. The streetlights turned smoggy, the moon blurred. People and cars were outlines of colour—red, dark blue and black. He caught snippets of phone calls from teenagers to their girlfriends. He crossed his ankles together, hugged his bag tighter to his belly. Someone else missed their bus. They waited near the lopsided trashcan at the bus stop, lighting up a cigarette. Familiar neon numbers loomed closer, his bus halted to a crawl while its doors fanned open. He stood up, feeling the ache in his hips as he boarded the bus. He would have to sit back down again to get rid of the ache.

He thought about what he had done that day and found that he could not remember. What had he eaten for lunch? How many cups of water had he drunk? Whom had he spoken with? Pedestrian questions trawled past him as he looked out the bus windows, pushing his spectacles up again with his left sleeve. The trees outside seemed to zoom past. Other passengers entered with the faces of those stuck in a long queue. He tried to go through the questions in his mind again, but he had forgotten what he wanted to remember. He alighted with a sigh, feeling the quick, hard pain pierce his feet again, this time also chafing the back where his shoe line ended. He pulled down his socks.

He walked past the playground as he made his way home. At night, it looked like a place of forbidden secrets. The swings could be haunted, the slide appeared more sinister. Yet it also roused a thrill in him. He could lie in the tube of the slide, sheltered, his desires safely hidden. An abrupt car drove past, shining its headlights near him. He put up his guard and quickened his steps. He tried again to think of what he had done for the day. How many times had he gone to the toilet? How much money was left in his EZ-Link card? Did he top it up? His mind drew a blank. The silence of the night asserted itself more. Lights were off in the neighbouring houses, and stray bats flew overhead in a burst of raucous shrills. The trees loomed large.

That was when he heard an ugly crack behind him, like that of finger joints snapping. He dragged his shoes to pause, trying to quieten his panting. He walked a little further on, careful to keep his pace without looking affected. Almost immediately, he heard a scuttling sound. It was scratchy and fleeting, a gravelly crunch. He held his bag to his stomach as he turned around. The pangolin caught sight of his swivel. It swiftly curled itself into a ball, its hide scraping against the road's stray rocks. He found himself surprised to be taken aback by the creature. Some time passed before it unfurled itself again, its armour glistening like the opal rind of a shell. It rocked itself the right side up, a gymnast completing a somersault.

He watched from a distance as it darted up a tree. He suddenly remembered he was nearing home. It was a Wednesday, and his wife would be out for dinner until late. He felt an old urge come over him, adrenaline rushing to his head after the sight of the pangolin. He continued to walk towards home with rapid steps. When he reached the gate, he smiled faintly to himself. Upon entering his house, he threw down his belongings on the couch after making sure that the door was locked. He made a beeline to his bedroom and removed all his clothes: the socks, one with a hole at the large toe, the black polyester trousers, the shirt yellowed at the collar and armpits. He stood in front of his wife's vanity table in his singlet and loose underwear. His movements began to change as he stripped the last two garments off.

He found the old rubbish bag shoved at the back of the closet. He took out his mother's beaded pastel pink dress, gently dusting off lint. He shook the dress out, hearing the rustling of beads like sliding sand in an hourglass. He took his time choosing a suitable bra and pair of panties from his wife's lingerie, deciding to go with a matching pale pink set. He donned them expertly, comfortably tethering the bra hook behind the folds of his back. He saw his belly jut out from above the panties and let out a giggle. The dress shimmied over his body like a gift slowly being placed in a parcel. He exhaled as he saw himself in the mirror, flushing a little at the jolt of the moment. The soft pink of the dress and underwear made him think of the exposed, vulnerable belly of the pangolin. He tenderly smoothed the dress down. He sat himself cross-legged at the vanity table, applying his make-up. At the same time, he wriggled his tired feet into a reliable pair of bedroom slippers.

Although it had been a while since he had last dressed up, his instincts sharpened as he contoured his face. He knew which shades and hues worked best for his bloodshot eyes, saggy jowls and sparse eyebrows. He thought about his mother working hard in the kitchen, wiping sweat off her left arm, wrinkling her nose a little at the stench of her armpits after a long day. He often sat on the bed, watching her become beautiful just for the sake of cheering herself up, cautiously asking her one day to let him try, feeling elated when she allowed him to as long as he did not tell his father. He tingled with excitement at the feel of his mother's too-big clothes and shoes, the rapt joy of looking graceful and enticing becoming a permissible world to him. At that time, he believed it was possible to be desired. He felt adored, seen and heard.

The crack of the pangolin's shell slapped him awake from his recollections. The same ugly sounds his father made on his back as he was getting caned, the same sound of his wife opening the door early, just as he was about to stand up and parade himself along the corridor of their tense house. She stared at him wanly. He forgot how to sit. He gripped the skirt of the dress, his fists clenched like the frightened ball of the pangolin. He wished for tough, impenetrable scales like the animal to ward off whatever came before and would continue to come next: his father's scathing disapproval, his wife's silent shame cocooned in the foetus of their unborn child. He heard his wife string tuneless sentences, in tandem with his pointless daily ruminations. What if he turns out like you? Did you spare a thought for me? What is the point of our marriage?

He turned to face himself in the mirror. The strokes of make-up now looked garish and crazed. He was out of shape and foolish in his mother's dress. A wretched sound rattled in his throat, like an animal wincing, caught in the dark of the night on a hostile road. He crumpled to the floor, realising that he could not dart up a tree or rock himself up to look at the room, right side up. He wondered if he looked like his mother when she sobbed. As the night stretched on, the pangolin rested snugly in the trenches of a guarded tree, its sturdy tail coiled around a large branch, protected like an untold secret.

16

No Place for Loneliness

Gargi Mehra

When the taxicab turned the corner, a cluster of buildings that resembled a tiered wedding cake rose before Ritesh's gaze. He sighed—if only he could live in an apartment complex as grand and beautiful. What a far cry from the suffocating one-bedroom apartment in Mumbai where he had so far lived with his parents.

To his intense surprise, the cabbie swerved right to the gate of the magnificent pink structures. Ritesh's mouth hung open to protest, to say that the man had committed a blunder. But then his eye caught the name 'Herman Park' and he just short of gasped.

While the driver extracted his luggage from the trunk, Ritesh disembarked like an automaton and counted out the cash, scarcely remembering to pocket the receipt as his colleagues in India had instructed him. The security guard at the gate demanded identification and, after squinting at Ritesh's passport, ushered him in.

A road wide enough to accommodate one car wound between the buildings, flanked by small gardens and barbecue areas on either side. Ritesh began his ascent and, a few minutes after sunrise, found himself wheeling his suitcase into the most spacious living room he had ever set his eyes upon.

The Amits, as he called the duo, welcomed him into their house. He had worked and partied with Amit S. and

Amit P. for more than five years in Mumbai, and counted them amongst his closest friends.

He glanced around the hall, wondering if he could play badminton if he erected a makeshift net, and decided he could—the only obstacle to a shuttlecock flying around the room lay in the form of a centrepiece that hung from the ceiling, which resembled an electrocuted crow. He'd have to take it down—he couldn't afford a showpiece that would scare away potential housemates, or even brides.

The Amits enquired after his journey, and Ritesh needed no more provocation to launch into his story. 'The flight was good but I watched a movie and it was very boring and on top of that I had to sit next to a newly married couple who were coming here on honeymoon, I think, but I wasn't sure ...'

They stood around in a circle, nodding noncommittally. Ritesh paused, sensing that they hovered on the cusp of something significant.

Amit P. cleared his throat. 'We have some news, actually. We've both got different assignments now, in the Dhoby Ghaut area. It's not far from the CBD—Central Business District.'

Ritesh nodded. 'Yes, I remember reading the full form of that abbreviation in the guidebook I got before leaving India. So that's good news for you, guys, but it means you have to commute there every day, right?'

Amit S. chimed in. 'Exactly, that's the point. We tried it and its forty-five to fifty minutes one way and standing in the MRT. Too much effort. So, we've found a nice HDB flat in Toa Payoh which is just a short, direct train ride from there.'

Ritesh fell silent. 'HDB is the Housing Development Board, right? The government housing?'

Amit P. nodded vigorously. 'That's right.'

'But how will this work out? It will be too expensive for me to pay the rent solo on this flat.'

'We can help you with that—in fact, we've already spread the message in our circles so you should get someone who will move in with you. We'll stay in touch.'

And before he could object any further, the boys had departed, taking their life with them in suitcases smaller than Ritesh had carried over the ocean. He slunk back onto the leather sofa, feeling sorry his friends had left before he could regale them with the details of his journey, starting from the moment his plane took off the tarmac at Mumbai and its subsequent arrival at Changi Airport five hours later.

The house shrank with their departure, the silence roaring in his ears. He drew the curtains open and a small balcony greeted him. But on the ground floor, he renounced any hopes of privacy.

He brewed himself a fresh cup of tea, the kind he'd have expected his wife to have made. At first, he fumbled while hunting for sugar but finally discovered it in a container labelled 'Coffee'. The view, even from the ground floor, was pleasing to the eye. But any modicum of privacy died a natural death with every passer-by who peeked into the house, glancing at the furnishings before settling on Ritesh nursing his cup. The women appeared to avert their gaze, but the men allowed their focus to linger almost aggressively before giving up and turning away.

Later he embarked upon a round of the house, taking in the decor. He turned away from the inert crow chandelier hanging in the middle of the hall and headed for the bedrooms.

His entire tiny flat in Mumbai might have fit into the room on the left. From its proportions Ritesh guessed it was the master bedroom. It boasted a dressing table, nightstand and en-suite bathroom. He hauled his suitcases into the room, stamping his ownership so that it remained out of bounds of potential flatmates.

He needed only one thing to spice up the prospect of living in the house—a woman, a partner he could share his life and his house with.

His first week flew past in a blur. He unpacked on Sunday and spent the day wandering the lanes of his new area, homing in on eateries that offered a huge variety of cuisines. On a sweaty Monday morning, he stood before the automatic glass doors that slid open to welcome him into the glass building that housed his new office. His new colleagues greeted him warmly, though after a few days he noticed their regrettable tendency to escape his clutches whenever he launched into a long, hearty tale about his travels.

Soon enough, he settled into a routine. He rose by seven each morning, setting the tea to boil before even brushing his teeth. He stood in the balcony, his fingers curled around the handle of the teacup, watching the women, young and old, pass by him as they circled the verdant condominium complex on their morning walk.

Every Friday he wedged himself into the social circle of his colleagues gathered around the water cooler and floated the idea of visiting a tourist spot. He poked and prodded at the politeness hanging in the air, and eventually stated it point-blank: if anyone wants to join me, you can. They all pleaded the same excuse: they had absorbed the sights and sounds of this island-nation many times over, having taken their relatives along as well. They had no wish to see them all over again. He nodded, pretending to understand their reasonable reasons. They mentioned nothing about avoiding his company, but he felt that unspoken message hang in the air. He taught himself to cook the meals that his wife, if he had one, might conjure up. Most evenings when he staggered home, he fixed a simple meal of dal and rice that lasted him at least two dinners. But some days he preferred the warmth of a restaurant or the bustle of a food court, and dined there straight after work, as he arrived at the MRT station. The sight of meat repulsed him, but he came upon dishes featuring mock duck and mock chicken. He resolved to open a restaurant back home in India that boasted these exotic items.

Everywhere he went, he marvelled at the women who rolled off the buses and trains. He gawked at their exquisite perfection, the glossiness of their skin, the sheen of their black hair, the flawless curvature of their skinny figures. They might have been twenty or sixty, but he could never guess.

On Saturdays he rode the bus to Mustafa Centre and loaded up on groceries for the week. On the office Intranet he put up a classified ad, circulating the message that he was looking for flatmates to share a spacious two-bedroom apartment. Several people responded but somehow no one ever showed up at his doorstep, even though he cited the Amits as his references.

He compiled a list of tourist spots and began with Jurong Bird Park. The list of places to visit and things to see dwindled.

One weekend he lay comatose on the sofa, idly browsing TV channels, when a knock at the door broke his chain of thought.

Two girls, or as he'd learnt to say in the corporate training, two women, stood at the door. The door had swung open and caught them mid-giggle. They looked quite young, at least a decade younger than him. One of them wore jeans and a simple blue top, the other was dressed in *salwar kameez*.[1]

'Yes?' he asked, sure they had got the wrong house.

'Are you Ritesh? We have come to see the house.'

'You mean … to stay here? As tenants?'

They nodded.

A myriad of thoughts invaded his mind, but he couldn't think of how to articulate them. For once in his life, words that usually tumbled out unbidden froze on his lips.

Unable to protest, he opened the door wide and let them in.

They entered and one of them gasped. 'What's that?'

She'd spotted the crow. Ritesh shrugged. 'It's part of the decor, an aesthetic piece of work.'

They stared at him. The jeans-clad girl nudged her. They looked around the hall. 'It's quite large.'

'Yes, but it's mostly empty. The relevant portion,' he pointed to the sofa and television set, 'is small.'

---

[1] Loose, pleated, pyjama-like trousers worn with a long shirt or tunic.

They looked at each other and then at him. 'Could we see the rooms?'

He showed them his room, opening the door only slightly. 'I've taken this room for myself as I came here first. It has an attached bathroom and dressing table, as you can see.'

They nodded but didn't seem perturbed.

The other room pleased them equally. 'It's nice and big,' remarked the jeans-clad girl.

'Yes, really nice. So, we can use the common bathroom, right?'

He nodded, wondering for the briefest of moments whom she really meant by 'we'.

They surveyed the large kitchen and small balcony beyond it that held the clothesline. He thanked his stars that he'd removed the clothes from there, else the girls would have had an eyeful of his underwear.

Eventually they left, giggling to each other.

He watched some shows absent-mindedly. As the screen blared, he pictured his life with two giggly girls. How would he greet them in the morning? What if they went around the house in their underwear? Or worse, in skimpy, provocative shorts? He couldn't allow it, but he wouldn't be able to bring himself to tell them off and forbid it either.

And where would they hang their clothes and underwear? He envisioned two pairs of synthetic domes jostling for prime space on the clothesline beside his boxer briefs. The thought alarmed him. Already the continuous rain on the island meant that clothes rarely dried fast, and he had to iron all his clothes more to keep them warm rather than render them flat and wearable.

The days passed by in a cycle of work and chores. He expected to hear that the girls would be ready to move in any day now, and thought he'd find them at his doorstep one morning, packed and ready with their suitcases.

When he grew tired of the tourist spots, when even the skyscrapers in the CBD failed to excite him and the vastness of the taxicabs no longer swallowed him whole, he abandoned them and zeroed in on the malls of Orchard Road. The beautiful, painted salesgirls plied him with a series of dresses and gowns for his imaginary bride. They even lured him in to try on full suit sets and let forth squeals of faux admiration when he emerged from the fitting room and they shrugged him into a blazer. He admired himself in the oblong full-length mirror. In Mumbai he had had few admirers, but clearly Singapore suited him much better. He wondered if one of the salesgirls might venture out for dinner with him, preferably at that new Indian buffet place. But back home he glimpsed his reflection in the mirror. The porcelain skin of those women would never suit the deep richness of his toffee-coloured complexion.

The next day he boarded a double-decker bus outside his condo and leaned back in his seat, watching the picturesque greenery of Singapore whiz past as he travelled to the other side of town. The new Apple store that had set up shop gave visitors a peek at the future. At the very least, Ritesh could induce some envy in his friends by putting up his photos both inside and outside it on Instagram and Facebook.

179

Outside the sky had become overcast. Clouds hung heavy and high, waiting to unleash a torrent.

While walking to the venue, he wondered if he shouldn't have stayed home and curled up in bed. But when he arrived at the floating dome, he goggled at it, and realised it was well worth it.

The dome floated in water, but he felt as if he himself must be walking upon water just like gods were known to do. When he entered the structure, he felt a kind of awe that he hadn't felt even inside the temple or Tirupati. But then, was that really fair to either the dome or the temple?

He walked around in a trance, gawking at the devices, wondering if he should actually seek out some advice on them. A group of avid Apple fanboys crowded around a Mac, ogling the screen as one young salesman put on a demo. Locals, Indians and a few white people formed part of the crowd. Every one of them hung on the words of the salesperson, as if the secrets of life and happiness were oozing from his lips.

A tinge of irritation descended on him. Everything in the work bespoke artifice. No true emotion lasted in any of the gamers or tech connoisseurs.

'It's all too much, isn't it?'

He swung around. It was the jeans-clad girl who had visited his house. He said, 'You know, I feel the fakeness of it all really gets to me sometimes.'

She stretched out a hand. 'You're Ritesh, right?'

His rough fingers met her shapely ones. 'Sorry, I've forgotten your name.'

'I'm Jeena, and this is Neelima. You remember, she had come with me that day?'

Neelima appeared by her side, wearing a *kurta* as she had done the first time too, a haversack perched upon her back just as before.

The words tumbled out before he could stop himself. 'I was thinking of having dinner at that new Indian restaurant nearby …'

They winced. Too expensive, they mumbled. He'd have to give them the other option.

'Or even the buffet place at Little India?'

That brightened them up.

'If you would like to join me …' He let his words float in the air, hoping the girls would pick up on the suggestion.

Jeena said, 'Good idea.'

Neelima nodded too. 'You know, actually, Amit told us you wouldn't welcome us into your house.'

This surprised Ritesh more than he had expected, but he contrived to maintain his composure. 'Did he give any reason why he thought so?'

She hesitated. 'Well, he said …'

He looked at her expectantly. 'Yes?'

'… that you were too conservative, and also that you talk too much.'

Jeena glanced at him. He had a strong feeling that she was scanning his face to note his reaction.

'I am disappointed, I must admit,' Ritesh said. 'They are not as good friends of mine as I thought them to be.'

Jeena said, 'Who needs them? You can always make new friends.'

He grinned. It was an agreeable suggestion. She returned it with a warm smile of her own.

Neelima said, 'Let's move. I'm hungry now.'

They fell in step alongside him. The now clear skies tempted them to walk.

An easy banter unravelled between them. For the first time, Ritesh felt he had come home.

IV

Home and Away

17

Rock

Dia Feng-Lowe

Moira Woo was, like so many young, carefree expats in Singapore, acclimatising to her new role of housewife, when X's text to her revealed the depth of lack in her life.

Until then, her Asian-American existence had been suburban, middle class and consistent although growing up, she had had an inkling that even with such cheerful origins something was vitally alien about her. She tried, unsuccessfully, all the usual tactics to fit in: cheerleading, skipping lunch, speaking only in school-hall slang. Her body was not built for grace, her mind not moulded to be sharp, however keenly aware she was of the ways she fell short as an immigrant child was not supposed to. Her parents scolded her for being a bamboo stick: segmented, neither here nor there. In desperation, they confiscated the landline in her room and doubled her weekend courses at the Chinese Cultural Centre next to the mall, a short drive away. They were relieved that she scraped into honour roll, that a proper university accepted her, that she graduated certified to teach. Teaching was a noble career, they told friends; really, she spent her days telling pesky children to take their fingers out of their nostrils.

Moira left university with another important asset: a steady boyfriend with good job prospects. She suspected that her parents, who at first bristled at his height, his frothy beard, his clumsiness with chopsticks, took to

Adam because of this. The next best thing to a daughter who was a doctor or a lawyer or an engineer was a daughter married to one. This point paid off for Moira, too: when an opportunity arose for Adam to work in Singapore, her parents were not reluctant to see her go, and she hitched herself to him like a one-way ticket out of her dead-end existence.

Soon, she found herself living in a gated residence by the ports, with guards, gardeners and a private elevator that whisked directly into her apartment. More luxury than she had allowed herself to imagine. The rent was unthinkably high but their combined income and desire for excitement emboldened them to take this leap.

She was good enough on appearance to secure a teaching job at a small international secondary school— her American accent exuded the confidence, education and sophistication that, as the elegant principal had said, parents and stakeholders deeply valued. She was not good enough, though, to keep the job past probation. Among the reasons given were that her work-visa sponsorship was too costly, and the school had been made aware of their requirement to hire locally. The reason she suspected: they mistook her Chinese skin tone, and thus her sensibilities, for their own and thought she would fit seamlessly into their system.

The job had gone to X or, rather, he had not been fired. Moira had noticed him on the first day, finding it odd that they, both new, held the same position and were brought in to co-teach. X was Singaporean-raised but trained abroad, the kind of Chinese boy her parents would have wanted as a son-in-law. He was boisterous where she was serious, confident where she was lost, and laughed from the depths of his core. He held himself like a star. The faculty gravitated to him, turning to him for lesson-planning tips, asking her what it was like to work with him. Truthfully, she had found his presence in the classroom with her, how he handled and guided the students like a symphony conductor, reassuring. They exchanged stolen glances when a student pulled an odd stunt. It was little wonder why he was chosen over her; she only wished she had known they were in competition.

What could she do now? Cosmopolitan women liked to live large—the endless hair and nail appointments, shopping sprees and champagne brunches—and she was an expat, no less, which should afford her a boost, at least, in the self-assurance that trivial spending was a personal right. But saving for a rainy day was laced into her identity; the momentary lapse of renting this apartment might just bring their downfall. *Would you look at that*, she thought, staring out the window on her first Monday as a housewife, at the well-kept gardens of lush jungle green, the sun's glare splitting perpetually in pool water. *Here comes rainy season.*

She was listless at breakfast. Adam didn't ask her what was wrong. Instead he smiled, cracked little jokes, offered advice: spruce up that resumé, trawl job sites and why not start a blog on how to save money? She was good at that.

'Or maybe I can take some time off. Get to know the city a bit more, you know? And be a ...' she cleared her throat theatrically, 'homemaker.' The notion jolted her. She, the child of an accountant and a shopkeeper, who had been conditioned to always be employed—a housewife. It felt excessive and scandalous, in the same way that this apartment was.

Adam chuckled. 'You need kids to be a homemaker. Honey, without kids, you're just deadbeat.'

Her breath hitched a little. At other times she might have extended the joke. Asked, *Well, wanna make some?* and tilted her head down and looked at him from over the top of her glasses in the way he said he liked. Adam smelled fresh and sweet from his aftershave, he was dressed for work already. He pushed his plate away, eyes fixed on his phone's screen. She shrugged to no one and picked up his breakfast things. Silently, she soaped and rinsed and wiped and fussed while he got ready to leave, giving her a peck on the cheek.

A muted ding from the elevator door shutting and Moira was all alone. He was under pressure at work and it was stressful, she told herself. He needed to be out in public, to have his guard up. She should be grateful that he was working so hard to provide for them. If the school didn't want her, if society didn't want her, then she should strive to at least feel comfortable and at ease in this apartment. At any rate, for now she could provide by cooking and cleaning. And then the text from X came, unexpected but timely as an intervention: *sry to disturb.. i noticed u left ur plant*

In her frenzy to vacate her space, she must have forgotten to take the little succulent sitting in a corner of her cubicle. She was surprised, meticulous as she was, that she hadn't remembered it at all.

Hi! she typed. Too bright but why put her shame on display? *Not sure I want to pick it up. Maybe you can water it for now?*

hey no prob.. will foster him for awhile

Moira paused at the tone. X had a playful charm, a way of talking that made you feel like the sun shone on you alone. Three flickering dots continued to appear on the screen. He was texting her, she realised with a slight warming of the cheeks, during the school day.

it'd be an honour to co-parent haha
Haha thanks!
hey. all for u

Moira felt a smile flood her face like a reflex. Was this more than platonic courtesy? She wasn't exactly bad to look at. Her features verged on pretty but for some unforgivable quirks: a narrow face and thin lips; slim ankles, big breasts overshadowed by a fleshy gut; eyes so wide, the whites so exposed around her murky irises, they gave her the expression of a terrified lizard. To others, she never gave off the impression of minding how she looked. Being hardworking had been her most winsome quality since her first boyfriend had told her that, unlike the prettier girls he'd dated, she 'tried hard'.

X saw past her diligence, perhaps, and uncovered a woman pleasing to the eye. Moira now recalled little things that she had noticed in his proximity and quickly dashed away, unsure of them. His way of leaning back in any chair as if he had no care in the world. The way he helped himself to leftover French fries from her plate without asking. That he was married but never brought up his wife or toddler in conversation. There were times when she walked with X through the school corridors, teaching material tucked under their arm, and she'd felt like the chosen one. He made her feel worldly. A natural woman.

Through texts throughout the day, X became a disembodied voice. How would he say these words he was writing to her now? He had a particular soft way of forming his vowels, like spring water rounding over pebbles, something soothing about his tone. He spoke like that during lessons and to her. But, out for lunch with the other teachers, after a few rounds of conversation, he would flip a switch to match their language, imbued with salted words and turns of phrase she had come to understand was Singlish. Fascinated yet inhibited, she would stop talking, not wanting to break the spell, like some ritual she had no business being at, unsure how to interject with her clumsy, brassy Americanness.

How would he say other words, dirty words, like 'caress' or 'moan' or 'fuck'? That last one would sound like a desired bruising.

Moira shook away the thought and stopped texting back. Attention from X created a small but intense flow radiating from the depths of her stomach. It gave her the pep to get on with the day and to do something nice for Adam. Dear Adam, toiling away for her. She owed him. She had never met anyone so mild and decent.

He came home later than usual that night, looking worn. Moira had experimented with a new recipe for homemade gnocchi with a salted egg carbonara. She found the recipe on a self-proclaimed 'yummy-mummy' blog run by a lawyer mother of three who grew her career as well as she did her kids and her garden of organic produce. The kind of superhero, overachieving woman, perfectly committed to public and private life, doting and doted on, that Moira had always expected to become. She could start by learning to cook more than the boiled pasta and sauce from a jar. They ate the first few mouthfuls in silence.

She wanted to know, though, and asked Adam sweetly how he liked the meal. He nodded thoughtfully.

'It's not great,' he said.

'It isn't?'

'There's no depth to the flavour.' He poked at the pale lumps. 'Maybe some taste at first but then, nothing. You didn't salt the gnocchi?'

'No.' Moira racked her brain. She had always been excellent at following instructions. 'The recipe didn't say to.'

'Is it not common sense?' he explained.

She gaped, but not visibly enough for him to notice. Early on during university, when they were just dating, she had opened the fridge for some yogurt and managed to shut the door on the carton. A sickening stream of curd had splattered on his kitchen walls and floor. Her stomach dropped and she froze momentarily, but Adam planted a kiss full on her lips and helped her clean up. Anytime her hip jutted into a table or a chair, she could still hear her lithe, petite mother tsking. He never seemed to notice. After their relationship's first flush, she saw him as a steady partner who would never fault her for little things. At their city-hall wedding he had called her lovely things, like smart, giving, kind and sweet. She had called him her rock.

The same Adam now said, 'Valiant effort, though.' The same Adam patted her arm, pushed his plate aside and smiled tightly. His face had grown heavier since their university days, but she knew his true smile still had a boyish quality that made his eyes twinkle. He went into the kitchen.

'Sorry if I seem off, work was a pain,' he called. 'Want a sandwich?'

She kept eating the gnocchi. 'What's going on?'

'Regular work stuff.' He raised his eyebrows at her and his smug, playful smile returned. 'No need for you to worry now that you're out of the game, hey?'

'Ha.' Her bite of gnocchi was too soft, and bland as padding. Her mouth swirled with saliva.

'You really don't have to keep eating that,' he said, as though he was the one who had poured his heart into making it.

'You can still tell me about work,' she managed to say. 'I can help.'

He talked vaguely about annoyances: who had an unsmiling demeanour, who acted too happy and who wanted to play matchmaker to every young person in the office. Moira packed the pasta down her gullet, determined not to leave leftovers.

A sharp, sudden pain lodged in her throat. A splinter of eggshell, she thought. It must have found its way in because of her shoddy cracking. Adam was still talking, and she didn't want him to know. She swallowed and swallowed until her esophagus clammed shut then reached for the water, but nothing helped. She smiled at him through the pain.

They were in bed by 10 pm. Humidity clung to their sheets, though a night breeze sloshed the water in the swimming pool so that it sounded like the sea. The sounds of crickets bothered Moira, like they were conspiring an invasion into her bed. She made herself as still as possible in order not to bother Adam, but he was sunken and still. A rock, indeed. There was no point in trying to fall asleep; loneliness padded her like thick cotton which she waded through, both feeling and not feeling her anger. Her ingratitude ached, too, a curious stabbing pain each time she swallowed until she remembered the eggshell. The beginning of tears prickled at her eyes.

Helplessness made for powerful motivation and relief surged like a drug when she picked up her phone. She was lucid enough to understand her intentions but not lucid enough to stop: *Hey! I want to get the plant! But I don't want to come to school. Shall we go for a walk?* Letters materialised under the guidance of fingers that had a will of their own. Was she really going through with this? She imagined floral arbours, thick curtain of magentas and wild tendrils, bodies meshed together. Her body, desired. *Maybe the Botanic Gardens?*

She read and re-read the texts they had exchanged earlier. His were either good-natured remarks or a compliment, there was no way of telling. The words laid flat on her screen. But X would surely see her late-night signal and understand that she could match him fully. He'd know that she could be the sexy, daring sort of woman if only she had someone who wanted to play this game too. Moira pressed the phone to her chest, as if the texts might flutter away. After a while, her head cleared, her breathing became shallow and regular. For the first time in a long time, she slept a dreamless night.

She awoke alone in bed to an early morning's powder blue and found texts delivered throughout the night: *oh i see! absence making the heart grow fonder?*

This had come hours after she had fallen asleep. A few minutes later, another text was sent: *oh dear, school's getting hectic. meetings, conferences, parent luncheons all coming up. aren't u glad ur gone lol*

Another one followed, not long after. *so i don't think i can meet. but i can leave it at reception?*

And the final blow: *will let u know of changes! praying for a Moira-cle ha!*

The words were, as always, friendly, playful and attentive, but the tone was unmistakable: palpable pity.

Moira felt the wobbling, stomach-dropping sensation she always did when she tripped or bumped into anything and waited for someone to tell her off. A split-second of in-between, uncertain time where she felt the most untethered. The most unwanted girl in the world.

But no one here could judge her; the only one who could, who had politely but categorically declined her advances, existed in a virtual world beyond her apartment. Out her bedroom window, activity flowed through people on the go: professionals with laptop cases looking hassled, tired helpers walking their employer's dogs, even the old, paunchy man secretly smoking his morning cigarette in a courtyard corner. Their lives laid defenceless against the effects of external elements. But couldn't hers be different? Inside her home, couldn't she fabricate whom she wanted to be, outside the judgement of others? Of course, concessions needed to be made. Without another thought, she exorcised the texts and the phone number. No one else within these walls needed to know.

Adam's voice filtered into her thoughts. In the kitchen, she found cabinets flung open, Adam, on his toes, reaching up.

'What's going on?'

'We're out of coffee,' he said to the cabinets, 'but I swear we had back-ups somewhere.'

She went into their bomb shelter, rummaged for the canister, tumbled a stack of canned soup in the process but returned to the kitchen and handed the coffee to him.

He looked surprised at first and then his face flushed with pleasure. 'What would I do without you?'

This was her cue. Moira made herself smile and, as if clicking the final tumbler into place and unlocking a secret garden that she could sculpt and fashion only for her, felt what genuine beaming comfort must be like. How perfectly nice this was, she thought, how mistaken she had been, how kind his personality, how solid like a rock. The sun was shining through the window.

18

Rediscovering the Familiar

Isha B.

'Welcome to Singapore, ladies and gentlemen, and to all Singaporeans and residents of Singapore, a very warm welcome home.'

I looked around me, searching for clues from the faces of my fellow passengers who had been on the same Singapore Airlines flight as me from London. Is this home for them? Do they all also have the red passport? My relationship with 'home' felt like an estranged one.

Having lived abroad for close to ten years, I felt the weight of that announcement on landing that day. Unlike previous trips, I had no plans to be back at the airport in a few weeks for a flight out again. Singapore was my permanent stop. That was, at least, my intent.

I missed my family. Bouts of loneliness abroad and a job offer back in Singapore spurred my decision to return.

'What time is breakfast today?'

The various dishes on the dinner table seemed to stare at my family and I, as we waited patiently for the call to prayer to signify the time to break fast. I could feel my stomach rumbling. The aroma of spices had filled the apartment earlier in the day as Mum busied herself in the kitchen. As it was the last day of the Ramadan fasting month, Mum cooked Eid dishes to send a few to Grandma that evening. Dinner was a rich feast, one that I had not partaken of in many years.

'*Allahu Akbar, Allahu Akbar* ...' The melodious *azan*[1] streamed from the radio on Warna 94.2 FM, the de facto Malay-Muslim free-to-air national radio station in Singapore.

I thought of my Ramadan days abroad when I broke fast mostly alone or with a few friends on selected days. Instead of awaiting any *azan* broadcast, my friends and I would constantly check the time on our phones. My poor cooking skills and the lack of Malay dishes at restaurants abroad also led to few Malay dishes finding their way to my dinner table. Middle Eastern food tended to be the usual *iftar*[2] dinner food overseas.

Ayam masak merah[3] and *rendang*[4] were amongst my favourite Eid dishes. That first Eid meal back home felt heavenly.

'Could you help me iron your brother's Eid clothes later tonight?' Mum asked during dinner. My brother smirked.

'K has hands and can do the ironing. I am expected to iron my Eid clothes. He can do the same!' I felt the swelling anger. My joy at the beginning of dinner had dissipated. I was tired of being portrayed as the 'unhelpful daughter' when my mother's actions bred the 'lazy-son' entitled attitude.

'It is fine if you cannot help me. You do not need to shout,' Mum said, shaking her head while looking at my father.

---

[1] Islamic call to prayer.

[2] Breakfast.

[3] Chicken in spicy tomato sauce.

[4] Spicy meat dish.

The dinner conversation shifted towards the planning of the Eid activities with relatives.

I remained annoyed as I helped Mum with the usual routine of clearing the plates after dinner, while my brother and father watched television.

When I began applying for jobs, another glaring adjustment came to head. I was appalled that Human Resources departments in Singapore considered information of race and religion as mandatory requirements to be submitted for job applications. A few even insisted that I provide a photograph of myself before my application could be forwarded to hiring managers.

At work, comments from colleagues annoyed me.

'Oh, you are Muslim and need to eat "halal"? But I thought you are more modern since you lived abroad. So you do not drink also?'

'Eh, not very team player of you *ah* to not join in team-building activities. You did not attend the Chinese New Year Yusheng get-together and the meet-up after work for drinks.'[5]

I did, however, learn the art of nodding and fake-smiling while partially registering the annoying comments. Being a little deaf helped my sanity at work.

'Auntie N! Look at my crown! I'm a princess,' my three-year-old niece cried out as she burst in through the front door. My brother trailed behind her while holding his other daughter. Seeing my nieces made me smile and I

---

[5] *Yusheng* or Prosperity Toss is a Cantonese-style raw fish salad. It usually consists of strips of raw fish mixed with shredded vegetables and a variety of sauces and condiments, among other ingredients.

felt thankful for being in Singapore with them. Watching my brother being a father to two young girls warmed my heart.

I hugged my niece as she told me how she got her crown, before running off to the playroom in the house with her sister.

'L watches too many princess shows with her. Can you balance things out?' my brother spoke to me later, commenting on his wife. It was Sunday and she was out with her friends while he took care of the kids that day.

I sneered, and reminded him of what an ass he had been to me when Mum tried to enforce traditional roles on me.

He rolled his eyes. 'Being a princess is not a traditional role,' he argued. 'I just want her to be able to also fend for herself.'

That afternoon, we watched the cartoon *Mulan* together with my nieces over dinner. My brother animatedly described the brave Mulan to his daughters, and how she outsmarted the other men. Later in the evening, my older niece was learning simple karate moves from my brother—moves which my brother only learned from watching the movie *Karate Kid*. Mr Miyage imparted memorable skills when we were growing up.

As I watched my brother playing with my niece, I looked at my younger niece who was sleeping peacefully next to me. Mum was in the kitchen cleaning up and doing the dishes while my father was watching television. Both my parents moulded into their respective roles based on what they knew at the time. Mum taught me what she knew based on what she understood to be important. I could not fault my parents.

'How is life?!' my friend Steph screeched via Zoom. In this new COVID normal, I had to make do with 'seeing' Steph simply via the computer screen. She was my closest friend from college, and when I had moved back to Singapore, we had planned to take regular trips every one to two years together. Last year we had travelled to Cambodia and I had planned to meet her in California this year for my holidays.

'Home is growing on me. And the COVID lockdown forced me to strike a balance with my parents in the house,' I said.

'I love your mum. I'm still reminded of how she took me sightseeing the last time I was in Singapore, and you were busy at work,' Steph said. And the feelings had been mutual, as Mum enjoyed her time with Steph, especially because Steph loved cooking and food. Mum had tried repeatedly to discuss recipes with me, but I never evinced any interest. At a restaurant, she and my brother would discuss the ingredients used in the dish while I was content with just eating. My motto, with regard to food, had always been 'Eat to Live' and not 'Live to Eat'.

'My mum probably wishes you were the daughter instead. I think I'm kind of useless in her eyes since I cannot cook, am typically messy and have poor cleaning skills,' I remarked in an off-handed manner.

'You're kidding! Did I not tell you the time when I had lunch with her? She shared how you left for overseas at seventeen, and how she supported you going even though you are the only daughter. She sounded proud of you and of herself for making decisions which I think might not have been the norm for most people in her situation. She might just be the typical Asian mum who will not say how proud she is of you in front of you,' Steph said.

I laughed. I was in my mid-thirties yet I was only starting to understand how my mother had felt during those years.

'I guess we all have our own mum issues, and I have COVID to thank for "forcing" me to now be home more often,' I said.

At the time, Singapore's circuit breaker was at its tail end while the number of infected people was skyrocketing in the United States, where Steph was living. I commented how Americans took the term 'freedom of choice' to another level with the optional wearing of masks during a pandemic.

'I guess you're relieved being in efficient, practical Singapore during this period,' Steph said.

'We are great followers. My boss eventually allowed for remote working only recently, after our prime minister recommended all employers to do that as the default option,' I said, knowing that Steph's company had allowed for remote working many months earlier. Face time remained a big deal in Singapore and many bosses, similar to mine, were afraid of a dip in productivity if employees were allowed to work from home. I felt that if remote working became more of a norm within the working world in Singapore, more mothers might be able to return to the workforce with the comfort of mind that they would be able to watch over their little ones. Fathers might also be able to help their wives balance out the household or childcare work while being home on certain days.

'The grass always seems greener on the other side!' Steph philosophically stated.

It was nearing the five-year mark since I had decided to return home. I had intended to mark this milestone by returning for a short holiday to my former 'home' in the US. But COVID-19 forced me to stay put, and perhaps that push was the 'full home immersion' I had needed. Even though I had returned to Singapore I had always been on the escape route, with overseas vacation trips planned every few months to leave the imagined sterility around me. But now, being home for an extended period encouraged me to focus my lens on the pluses surrounding me and to search for the beauty within my home, such as the generosity of Singaporeans coming together during the pandemic. The rough edges still existed; Singapore was a home that was not perfect but one that I hoped would evolve for the better. And by planting my roots more permanently, with the purchase of my signature built-to-order HDB flat next year as I turned thirty-five, I wanted to continue being part of the journey of rediscovering my home.

19

A Bold Crossover

(The ABC of a New Beginning)

Azeena Badarudeen

'Dear Ms Alyna, you are just one step away from being a proud homeowner! Click on the "Submit" button to secure your application for Block 101, Seng Kang Avenue 11 #11-111 Singapore 111101!'

I twiddled with my phone, fully conscious of what I was attempting to plunge into while simultaneously uncertain about what this decision would entail for the only other person I knew so well in all of my thirty-five years: my mother Sulekha.

My decade-long presence on matchmaking websites from the time I returned to Singapore following the completion of my undergraduate education in journalism at New York University had borne no fruit, leaving both my mother and I several thousand dollars poorer and, needless to say, bitter and angry at each other over who was the primary contributor to this prolonged failure. Chafed at her family for ostracising her after she had eloped to marry my father following their whirlwind romance in the 1980s, my mother was resolute about conducting a wedding so grand for me that it would be the talk of the town. My grandparents could never come to terms with the fact their youngest child and only daughter would cross the line by being bold enough to choose her own groom, an unemployed man nine years her senior. They had harboured dreams of witnessing her wedding being conducted in full view of their community folk settled in Singapore, fellow Keralites who had made their way to the shores of Singapore on the deck of the SS *Rajulah* and, more importantly, to a boy *they had picked*, the ultimate litmus test of any child's filial piety in their opinion. Who was to know that sending their attractive twenty-one-year-old to evening typing classes would bring so much anguish to their otherwise peaceful life? Yet, nothing could precede the place that honour had in the Seletar Hills home Sulekha grew up in. Hence, following her decision to marry Niran, she left home, for there was no redemption for a lost reputation in the conservative community she grew up in.

I grew up never really knowing my father. My only knowledge of him were his name and NRIC number on my birth certificate. All photographs of him and with him were duly destroyed the moment my mother realised that my father was never serious about honouring his promise of looking for a job. When I turned three, my mother duly removed his name from mine through a deed poll. She did not see the need for me to be acknowledged as the 'D(aughter)/O(f)'such an individual. Having been ostracised by her family meant that my mother had to independently look for solutions to problems associated with daily such as repairing a fused bulb or a leaking faucet. The meagre monthly salary she drew as an administrative assistant with an insurance company deemed plumbing and electrician services as luxuries we could ill-afford. My mother, as prideful as her parents who had disowned her, refused to seek help from them or her six older brothers or anyone she had been acquainted with in her pre-motherhood days.

The combination of pride and embarrassment from having made the wrong decision about her spouse gave birth to a new tenacity in my mother, which gave her the strength to single-handedly go through the entire home purchase and renovation processes. Aah, after spending the first six years of my life shuttling from room to room in different HDB flats, we finally had our own home, a two-room HDB flat just a stone's throw away from Toa Payoh MRT station. I was thrust into independence instantly, learning the ropes of basic cooking and the art of sharing household chores. We never had visitors over, neither relatives nor friends. Growing up, I sensed that questions about whether my classmates could come to our place would be sensitive and hence went through my entire academic career steering clear of conversations that would lead to such requests. Home was an imagined space with my parents and myself as I had always depicted in the essays and journal entries I submitted to my teacher in my primary-school days. Before long, I figured out that only pupils who were mischievous or fared poorly in their school work and examinations would have teachers hauling their parents over at Meet-the-Parents sessions. Perhaps it was my grandparents' dominance and mother's pride in me that I began working very hard in school and put on my best behaviour at all times, all because it meant that my teachers would never have to meet my mother and discover the complexity of our domestic existence.

I rarely had any friends, choosing to mingle with everyone cordially, establishing contact sufficient to identify me but insufficient to know *who* I was. Our Toa Payoh home soon became a refuge for me to emotionally release myself in the brief periods before my mother returned home from work, careful about not letting her see my tears. I never truly felt a connection to the address that my NRIC bore simply because I had no real memories created that I could safely deposit in my repository of long-term memories, stories that could be passed on to the next generation. Thus, the bond-free scholarship to pursue journalism at New York University after obtaining stellar results at the GCE A-levels came as a much-needed respite to rediscover who I was and where I truly belonged. However, during my four years at university, I found myself falling into the same patterns of social isolation and immersion in work, hardly making any true connections by the time I had to leave for Singapore. I did not visit home throughout my undergraduate years, unlike the rest of my fellow Singaporeans, because I was not even sure if I had fully grasped the essence of what that word meant.

My mother's receipt of my arrival back home was lukewarm. Like me, she too found ways to keep herself occupied with work and home. She had already clocked in twenty-five years of service at the insurance company she had first found employment at and was now administrative manager. With a higher paycheck, she set aside some funds for her retirement and purchased some gold jewellery for the wedding she was planning for me, something she never explicitly discussed with me but which I always knew was at the forefront of her thoughts.

She had been determined to educate me well, at least well enough to surpass her own educational qualifications and, beyond that, arrange my marriage to a professionally qualified groom who was faring well in his career in what I always felt was an attempt at fulfilling *her* parents' dreams and salvaging the family reputation that she had marred as a result of her hasty actions. As her only child and out of obligatory gratitude for providing me with a home and all else needed for survival, I did not resist when she brought me to various studios for makeover photoshoots to make me 'matrimony-ready' for the profiles she had created for me on numerous matchmaking websites. Many profiles 'matched me perfectly' in terms of qualifications and career aspirations but the biggest stumbling blocks came when I was asked about my father and if I would be willing to move overseas, leaving behind my mother. Until then, the thought of leaving home never struck me. I had always assumed that things would always remain the same and if changes were to occur, as they would since the course of life is always subject to the forces of fate, destiny and circumstances, I would somehow embrace them.

Unanswered questions about my father and my willingness to move abroad caused many prospective grooms to soon lose interest in my profile. Unlike in the 1980s, when suitors would visit the homes of prospective brides, there was no way in which my mother and I could get these would-be spouses to do the same. The Internet, despite its power of easily concealing the gulf created by physical distance, simply could not create the connection that sparks between individuals meeting face to face. Alas, an entire decade went by without any success on the matrimonial front. My mother, frustrated at how things had evolved, began blaming my introverted nature for the unsuccessful attempts at entering matrimonial union. Years of pent-up frustration began to create tension between us, especially when I started retorting with how she had brought this fate upon me by depriving me of a proper home to grow up in and, worse still, for having incurred the wrath of her parents and bringing shame to her home, the consequence of her youthful folly.

I was now thirty-four and the stark realisation that I had only a year before my thirty-fifth birthday, which would render me eligible for the purchase of my own HDB home, dawned on me. I was exhausted with the emotional emptiness I had endured for almost three decades and seriously began courting the idea of getting my own home, a space that would be mine, one that reflected what mattered the most to me. The prospect of leaving the only person I had shared my entire life with seemed daunting and ironically lonely, given that being with her in an emotionally void coexistence was the very source of my own loneliness.

I reflected deeply on the twenty-eight years I had spent in our two-room Toa Payoh flat. I had gone to schools within the vicinity throughout my entire school life, moving abroad temporarily only to attend university. Upon my return following my graduation in mid-2010, I had found employment as an editor for a company in Bishan, which was only two MRT stops from Toa Payoh and within the ambit of the North-South MRT line. My mother too never had to cross lines, having found employment at an insurance company situated in Toa Payoh from the time we had moved here.

Did I like living here? I thought about all the weekends I had wordlessly accompanied my mother to the NTUC supermarket situated in the basement of Toa Payoh MRT station to purchase our weekly groceries. Our interactions were mostly functional, me stretching my hands to collect some of the plastic bags from the cashier and when I began earning, quickly offering to pay the bill once the cashier had tallied the price of all the items. We hardly went out for 'fun' either together or with our colleagues. We had both systematically found ways to avoid events that encouraged staff to bring family members and only attended gatherings which were large in scale so that slipping out unnoticed and mumbling a 'I've got something urgent to attend to', to anyone whom we had the misfortune of bumping into either of us was all that was needed to account for our truncated attendance.

Home had always been a functional space and its maintenance had been neatly segregated into the tasks we shared between us. As I grew up, gaining in physical strength and stature, I took over some of the more challenging household chores like hanging out the laundry and mopping the flat. My mother hardly asked if I could help her primarily because our unspoken exchanges were often sufficient in conveying what the other needed or wanted. In the absence of male family members who could have potentially taken on such physically demanding tasks, I always wondered how my grandparents and six maternal uncles were and if they ever thought of us but never mustered up the courage to ask my mother about them for fear of triggering memories of a painful past tainted with shame, humiliation and bittersweet memories. I never demonstrated an interest in maintaining social-media accounts, thus automatically eliminating the option of tracing estranged extended family members virtually as some individuals have done since the advent of social-media platforms at the turn of the new millennium.

But the amalgamation of boredom, loneliness and emptiness were beginning to gnaw at me from within since I turned thirty-four. I knew I had to carve a life out for myself sooner rather than later. So, I embarked on my HDB flat search which culminated in finding a unit that I really liked exactly a week after I had turned thirty-five. I was desperate to create new memories, whatever they might be and whomever they may be with and knew that the best way to do so was to find my sense of place in a new space, devoid of all bias. I made the bold and unthinkable move of selecting a flat in a neighbourhood on a different MRT line. My choice meant I would be crossing lines for the first time in my life. For someone who had lived her entire life in the full consciousness of how her actions would impact the feelings of the only kin she knew, it felt strange to be making a decision for myself that my mother had no knowledge of.

I stared at the 'Submit' button on the HDB resale flat application page. I still had a good two minutes before my session timed out, despite having been deep in thought for what seemed like an eternity. There was no need to contemplate any further. I was clear about crossing new lines and was learning the ABC of doing so.

20

Locomoting

Vanessa Ng Q.R.

Familiarity

(n.) A concept that inverses over time.

Example: After staying in that room for a decade, I forgot
how it looked. The off-white walls seemed yellower than
I recalled, with splatters of paint cracks at the corners
staring back at me. I have habitually overlooked this
area in my regime to solidify a sense of familiarity. This
beautiful space now appears foreign upon scrutiny.

Mason was packing boxes. He had been hunched over,
organising countless paper things into bigger paper
structures for the past two hours. Tomorrow, he would
need to sign more papers and dish out, surprise, surprise,
more hard-earned papers to get everything delivered to
his new home.

There had been many exchanges of thin pulp wafers
these days.

In primary school, Mason learnt that everything on
earth belongs to one of three distinct categories—alive,
once alive or never alive. This was before matters got
more complicated, and things had to be forced into tiers
on a hierarchical chain. Before all that complexity seeped
in, though, life was simple. So simple that all the wooden
furniture, cupboard of books and photo albums would

have simply been labelled 'once alive'. All these were just different versions of trees which once stood tall, breathing. Instead, Mason had to purchase paper sticker labels to separate these items into 'bedroom: furniture', 'study room: fiction books' and more.

Mason's back was having a hard time. He had already signed up for stiff shoulders, neck and back after settling for a desk-bound job, but this was something else. It was sheer back-breaking manual labour that his unfit self could not put up with. His friends had volunteered to help but Mason had refused, insisting that he could cope. The truth was that he could, indeed, cope. But it was a difficult sort of coping, and Mason wished that he had taken his friends up on their offer.

Remembering the instructor from his first and last yoga class, Mason stretched as best as he could and felt a little better. He wondered if he should sign up for a trial class at a yoga studio near his new place.

Mason laid flat on the wooden floor, as flat as he could, anyway. He angled his body to fit whatever little floor space was left, with piles of boxes and dust everywhere. Despite having a sensitive nose, Mason did not sneeze. This was coming from someone with a sinus, who teared at mild perfume fragrances, distant cigarette smoke and medical ointment. He had gotten used to dust just from a week of packing. Imagine what biological feats he could achieve if he just forced himself into accepting things.

Staring at the ceiling, Mason felt a tad out of place in his decade-old bedroom. He knew shifting to a larger house with more amenities would be great, but was this all necessary? Did he actually need a new residence? The new home was a twenty-minute drive away, so it was not exactly a huge change. This was Singapore, after all, the little red dot with everything close to everything else.

Mason had treated this move as a milestone event, a harbinger of greater things in life and a wondrous start to a magical future. Shifting to a new abode puts people in a new head space. Old memories fade over time when nestled in our brains, but get well preserved when tied to a physical space. This also explains why you tend to forget what you were supposed to do when you exit a room. After leaving the door frame, you leave your compartmentalised memory behind in the room that you have exited from. Once Mason left his HDB apartment, his brain would be rewired to do a whole new set of things. He knew that and was excited for it.

At the same time, Mason was certain that his already forgetful self would probably never be able to relive this moment ever again. He wondered if the new homeowners would allow him to visit his old bedroom every five years to relive some of his space-dependent memories accurately, and shrugged this idea off. How would he even bring it up to the strangers who would now occupy his dwelling?

This well-worn area had provided much solace to Mason over the years. It was more than just a tiny unit parked within a high-rise building of precast and stackable blocks dumped and gelled together quickly. It was a place he had spent actual time in.

Mason stood up, and walked out to the living room. The colour of the wall seemed a little off. It was supposed to be of a light shade of blue that seemed almost white, but it appeared kind of yellowish now.

Perhaps it was the lights that Mason had randomly picked off the shelves last year that gave the walls this dirty tinge. He should have just given the walls a new coat of paint three years ago when his friend got into the renovation business and wanted to sell him something. Mason was not sure what his friend wanted to sell him. Maybe he would have remembered if he did not put up such high walls around himself during the sales pitch. He had always had a knack for blocking things out, and had built his own method of noise cancellation, devoid of unnecessary emotions. That was, after all, the most efficient way to cope.

Mason sat down on the leather sofa. He patted the seat twice out of habit before sitting down. It was made of real leather, the salesperson had assured him, and would last long and be airy enough. It seemed pretty accurate so far, but that might have been caused by the jade cover that his father had got him. Mason had been sitting on little plates of jade sewn together into a blanket for years. They were supposed to keep him cool in Singapore's tropical climate. His father was also the one who insisted on him getting a leather sofa as opposed to a much cheaper plastic one although Mason really could not be bothered about how warm his buttocks would feel during the hotter months. The country was hot, period, and the only way to stay cool was to blast the fan, turn on the air-conditioner or move to a different country. Mason had actually considered the final option but decided that he should stay here, close to his parents.

The boy missed living with his parents as he did when he was younger. There were a variety of yells exchanged and muttered curses during the period, which were accompanied by doors slammed and painful tolerance. However, there were enough positive and heart-warming times as well to make him miss the old days. It was both a place of refuge and source of pain. Would he shift back in? No. Did he miss the old times? Yes. That was the relationship that he had with his parents.

The family communicated in unconventionally quiet ways, which was not at all conducive to expressing love or concern when living separately. Mason knew he would bring the sofa and jade cover to his new home to add some familiarity to an otherwise alien space. His parents would perform the standard pineapple-rolling ceremony in his new home to bring in good luck, anyway, and would be happy to see this in the new apartment. That would be a source of conversation that he could expand over lunch with Pa and Ma. Mason made a mental shortlist of nice restaurants to bring his parents to, and planned some excuses about winning the lottery or getting promoted so that his parents would not complain about the overpriced food.

Mason massaged his neck briefly and looked around the sloppy living room. Unlike other messy people, he had no sense of organisation within the chaos. It was disordered because he was lazy, and he could never find anything that he was looking for.

This phenomenon extended to his career and relationship. He was always searching for things he had owned, but misplaced due to neglect. As time passed, he could no longer find anything anymore, and simply stuck to getting new things while the clutter built up and enveloped him. This was probably one of the reasons why Mason wanted to get a new house. He would have no choice but to sort out the mess, and hopefully be able to find all the things he was looking for. A new start would make this process less difficult and provide a semblance of structure, Mason thought.

Amidst the disorder, something caught his eye. A shoebox lay on the table, dug out of one of the many drawers that Mason had conveniently forgotten about. It was filled with strange bottlecaps, arcade tokens and membership cards to places he could not remember visiting. A couple of old diskettes or floppy disks sat at the bottom of the shoebox, containing contents that Mason would never get to find out because nobody owned the file reader anymore. More importantly, there were letters from friends and past girlfriends penned with faded ink, as well as shabbily cut photographs of his childhood. There was even a three-line, short confessional poem from a girl in kindergarten that he had kept. He chuckled and wondered how everyone was doing.

Mason was not at all stressed about the move. In fact, he had always been comfortable with changes and transitions. For as long as he could remember, he was in flux and had never lived in a state of permanence. As a child, he travelled to wherever his parents worked. At university, he studied abroad and went on multiple exchange trips. At work, he travelled out of Singapore extensively. Mason was a global citizen who fit in everywhere but never truly belonged.

Today, however, was different. He had quit his work and started at a local firm with no overseas clients or branches. His new forever apartment awaited him, welcoming him after a fortune spent on renovations. Mason was determined to stop locomoting, and to stay fixed in a place for a change. He bought some gifts for his future neighbours and even rehearsed what he was going to say to facilitate the greeting process. That was how committed Mason was to staying grounded in a perpetual place of residence.

Over the past week or so, he understood that while being able to adapt to change was one of his greatest traits, it was not something that he enjoyed doing. This was difficult for Mason to admit to, as he had spent years conditioning himself that he loved being all over the place. He told himself that it was enjoyable being able to blend in everywhere. That must be true, for the praise he had received throughout his life had revolved around his ability to adapt. After all, how many people could say that they had travelled all over the world and lived in multiple cultures? He was always deemed the cool kid and now, the adult leading a dream life. But was he genuinely happy?

Mason had spent his whole life thinking he loved change. He took pride in challenging himself, and accustomed himself to doing so by continuously being on his toes in a new environment. He never stopped to smell the flowers, and just kept moving. Now that Mason had taken the first step to admitting that he hated what he was used to doing for decades, he could finally relax in a comfortable space. This shift would put a stop to all other changes, and there would no longer be any need to step out of his comfort zone. Living in his own little bubble would be a great change of pace, and a welcome one at that. Mason looked forward to freely redefining his likes and dislikes, and was excited to find a replacement hobby.

But for now, Mason had just a single task—to pack boxes. He got off the sofa and eyed the room. Most of the items had already been grouped or cleared, very much like his mental space.

Mason smiled, gave his body another good stretch, and continued placing paper things into bigger paper structures. Tomorrow, he would sign more papers with his favourite pen, and dish out hard-earned ones to get these boxes quickly delivered to his new home. And he simply could not wait.

21

Arriving

Arathi Devandran

The first time I left, my mother had just been diagnosed with breast cancer. We found out about her diagnosis and my move within weeks of each other.

The days leading up to my leaving were mechanical: long stretches in hospital waiting rooms as my mother went through cycle after cycle of chemotherapy, longer stretches into the nights filling up visa applications and other paperwork.

The whispers followed me relentlessly.

'What a selfish, ungrateful girl she is, leaving her mother when she needs her daughter the most,' murmured my mother's relatives, ever present in their disdain of my actions or their absence.

When I heard this, I wondered if they would have whispered differently of me if I had been a son instead of a daughter. The same relatives, some of whom had refused to acknowledge me when I was born—because I was a girl. The same relatives who only began to develop a relationship with me when it seemed I was heading towards a measure of success in my adulthood.

'Do you even know what you have signed up for? Are you ready to do this—pursue your dreams while being plagued by this guilt? Shouldn't you stay at home and be a good little girl?' taunted my own tortured mind.

Rationally, I knew being a woman had very little bearing on what I should and should not do. However, society's conditioning had been a constant reminder that I had responsibilities at home, for others, that my own needs and dreams could take a backseat.

And yet, I knew that if I did not take up this opportunity now, I would live a life tinged with regret.

I was nineteen when I left my ailing mother and my home to live abroad for the first time. I don't remember much about leaving, only that I was tired and overwhelmed by a grief that I could not fully articulate. All I wanted to do was to curl up in my window seat in the aeroplane and cry quietly to myself. It was a long and lonely plane ride.

It was also the beginning of a long, slow and painful struggle with my guilt and my perceived sense of place at home.

The first time I properly arrived home, three years later, I was 12 kilograms lighter, and felt about fifty years older. I had graduated only three weeks earlier and had barely been able to finish packing before I found myself back, perspiring profusely every time I stepped out, my accent tinged with something foreign.

The first thing I did when I came back was to get a haircut. I had spent three years dousing my head in chemicals to straighten my unruly curls and was done trying to make myself into someone that I was not. The straightened bits of my hair fell to the ground as the hairdresser doggedly pressed on. My curls sprang up anew and I looked at myself in the mirror and thought, 'Who are you and why have you returned?'

Being away had made my heart and mind grow in ways that seemed too big for my parents' three-room flat in the West.

I moved back into my old-new room and recognised nothing except my collection of books, which I had painstakingly added to over the years. My single bed was too small for me, even though I had not grown that much taller. Lying in bed, I watched the corridor lights twinkle against my stained-glass windows and waited for sleep to come; rest was increasingly elusive then. In the end, I would get out of bed at 4.30 am most mornings and jog around my estate, exploring the local park connectors in the darkness.

As I watched the sun rise by the *lonkang*[1] near my parents' home, the tightness in my chest would lessen. The photo gallery on my iPhone was filled with pictures of the sky, tracking the path of the light in the morning.

Looking back at my camera roll, it is clear to me that I was desperately searching for something familiar, something to anchor me, something to tell me that I had come back to the place I was meant to be in—my home.

I felt too big for my own skin, too much of an adult woman (whatever that meant), one who was starting to be set in her own ways and routines, and who felt increasingly stifled in a home where her parents could not understand that their daughter had changed, that she was no longer a child but almost an equal.

In the years that I had been away, I had gotten used to travelling on a whim. I travelled simply and usually alone.

---

[1] Canal.

I took weekend trips and longer holidays that spanned the weekdays. In my more nostalgic moments now, the memories return to me in flashes.

Barcelona, Paris, Vienna. Drinking local wine and eating lavender-flavoured ice cream. Discovering architecture that I had seen only in my dreams and dishes whose names I cannot pronounce to this day. Finding reading corners in planes, trains, buses and cabs.

Loughborough, Manchester, Birmingham. Walking along cobblestoned streets and staring into pretty storefronts decorated wildly for Christmas. Meandering through farmers' markets, marvelling at the earth's produce and abundance. Sitting in parks and filling the pages of my journal.

Those were simpler times and perhaps I had been a simpler person.

You see, I had convinced myself that if I left often enough, I would understand what it would mean to come back home. As if arriving home was a feeling waiting to be picked up, like the letters in my mailbox.

The permanence that characterised my return was unsettling. Some of it was forced upon me: I was now a working adult, and that meant I had professional responsibilities for which I had to turn up five days a week, several hours a day. I sat in front of a computer, talked to people and wrote e-mails. Often, I caught myself wondering how I had arrived at this place and whether this was the arrival I had envisioned for myself when I was younger.

By the time the weekend rolled around, I was usually too tired to do anything substantial. Living in the

West provided me with the physical distance from the humdrum of the city centre. We were surrounded by parks and hiking trails that gave me the space I needed from my Monday-to-Friday life.

Mostly I would hole myself up at home with my parents, read many books and stare out into our sprawling garden. During the years I had been away, my mum had channelled all the love she had for me into growing her urban garden. It was now a splendid thing, where we could harvest limes, mangoes and the occasional bunch of bananas. When the weather became unbearably warm, the neighbourhood cats would curl up in the shade provided by my mother's plants and snooze. Sometimes I could lure them out to play; usually, though, they ignored me. I would spend my afternoons sitting on the outside steps staring at them, idly wondering if I would ever have a cat of my own.

I was also lucky enough to have three of my closest friends living near me. Sometimes we would meet at the nearest suburban mall, trading stories about work and family over milk tea and toasted peanut butter sandwiches. On evenings where we were feeling particularly wild, we would head to a German bar for drinks and a good round of venting.

In this way, time passed. I stopped leaving, stayed in for the most part and rested. Until one day, I decided I had to do it again.

'Are you sure it's safe for a young girl like you to travel alone? What's so nice about travelling in a foreign country all by yourself?' The wagging tongues of my relatives never stopped.

'Why don't you stay at home and spend time with us? You're always out and about,' my mother would suggest. I did not realise then that my mother, in her own way, was trying to tell me that she missed me and was trying to grasp at anything that would remind her that the daughter she had said goodbye to all those years ago was still here somewhere.

You see, my mother had no idea what to do with this version of me—the more independent, self-assured, grown-up woman. By not being able to understand who I was, she was not able to understand her role and purpose in my life. What did being a mother to an adult woman look like? What were the boundaries that existed in the relationship? How much could she sway and influence my life without me pushing back, or ignoring her entirely? These were difficult questions, and my mother struggled to grapple with them.

Though we are markedly different in some ways, we are very similar in others. She had always expected me to be her perfect daughter and I had always expected her to be my perfect mother. In this foolishness our similarity was startling and, needless to say, only resulted in conflict brought about by misplaced expectations.

My mother's expectations of an adult daughter were a result of what she had seen and experienced in her life. I could not blame her for her beliefs but I had neither the grace nor the magnanimity at that age to be more patient with her. My expectations of my mother were heavily influenced by Anglophilic ideas that I had read and observed in my years abroad. I was still young and naïve, and perhaps more child than adult. I had neither the grace nor the patience to amicably discuss our different worldviews. Naturally, then, there was conflict. I found more and more reasons to leave often, to see the world, to escape the confines of womanhood that people were trying to place me in.

Eventually, I decided that I had to have my own home and my own space. I knew instinctively that this would change the dynamic of my relationship with my family drastically. Instead of taking each other's presence for granted, each meeting and reunion between us would become a choice that we had willingly made to spend time with each other. I also knew it would be hard for many reasons. Where I lived, renting was an anomaly; it was not altogether encouraged, and the options for a single young woman to rent a home were far and few between. I also knew that the same relatives who had complained about my filial lack would wag their tongues about my wayward behaviour; it meant little to me, but they were my parents' family and I am sure it would mean something to them. Then, of course, there were my parents themselves, who could not fully grasp the reasons behind my decision.

I did it anyway. I packed my meagre belongings in black bin bags and moved out of my parents' home into a tiny room in a different part of the city. It was situated on a high floor with large windows and I knew I could witness the sunrise every morning if I left the curtains undrawn.

The first day in my new home, I took a seat by the window and stared out into the sky.

So much of my arriving home has been characterised by my leaving and about understanding my role as a woman at home, in society.

I have wondered about this often. What has made me so uncomfortable in my own home that I have been seeking it outside? What do I want home to mean? I have learnt a few things over the years.

To understand that the expectations others place on us are a product of their own lived experiences and that, though they can be dealt with graciously and amicably, they should not morph into unrealistic cages within which we feel trapped. That growing up has to be characterised by empathy, grace and patience and that is what we must strive towards. That, ultimately, we owe it to ourselves to make the best of our lives, and that we must work towards that. That perhaps I must be content with this—finding a series of moments that make me feel like I am comfortable in a space, in myself and that, over time, these moments would add up to something bigger. Maybe if these moments stretch out long enough, they could last me a lifetime.

Something about this last lesson sits well with me, settles me. Which is why I have decided to leave again.

I am going to a place faraway, almost a different world. It is going to be a long journey and I am not certain when I will return.

This time, though, it feels less like fleeing and more like the gentle, conscious choice to honour change and acknowledge this passage of time. For once, I am curiously excited about coming back home, wherever that is, whenever that will be. I note this feeling, filing it away safely so that I can revisit it in my more untethered moments.

For now, I am getting ready to say goodbye. I take a deep breath and continue to pack my things.

About the Contributors

Isha B. works in project management. She started pursuing creative writing recently and has participated in various writing workshops in Singapore. As a new writer, she is still discovering her writing voice and style. She has grown up in the eastern part of Singapore her entire life. After living abroad for a while in the US and Canada, she returned home a few years ago.

Azeena Badarudeen is a third-generation Singaporean who spent her childhood and schooldays in Ang Mo Kio and Bishan. As a child growing up in an extended family in Singapore in the 1990s, she feasted on a diet of stories of her maternal family's time in Jalan Kayu as well as her paternal family's years in Varkala, southern Kerala. An avid reader, Sudha Murthy and Chitra Banerjee Divakaruni count among some of her favourite writers.

Ilya Katrinnada Binte Zubaidi has a background in anthropology, and her geeky interests lie in the intersections of creativity, community and education. She is particularly keen to learn more about cultural hybridities and post-disaster arts. Born and bred in the rather obscure and far-flung western end of Singapore, she enjoys expressing her thoughts through writing and photography.

Aparna Das Sadhukhan was born in Kolkata and raised in southern India, and currently lives in Singapore. She began her career as an advertising and communications professional to soon realise her true calling as a jewellery designer while living in Sydney, Australia. She ran a successful jewellery label, Nine by Thirty, for eleven years while quietly chasing her other calling as a writer. *Escape Routes* (2019), a self-published collection of her short stories, is her first book.

Arathi Devandran curates personal experiences, snapshots of the world and the stories people are willing to share with her through prose and poetry at www. miffalicious.com.

Dia Feng-Lowe is a writer and educator. A transplant, she currently resides in Singapore with her partner and, surrounded by potted houseplants, is beginning to feel at home herself. Her writing has appeared in *Flash Fiction Magazine* and *Merrimack Review*, among others.

Surinder Kaur was born and raised as a Singaporean Punjabi. Through her light-hearted stories, she reflects on the traditions and beliefs of her community and hopes to bring about appreciation of her roots.

Ken Lye completed his MA in Creative Writing in 2019, and his short stories have been selected by online literary journals in Singapore, China and Japan. He has also contributed articles on the Singapore arts scene to The Esplanade and various publications.

Cecilia Mahendran has had an interest in creative writing since her childhood. She writes as a hobby and has had her stories published in anthologies under Writing the City, a writing group, and on ReadFest website, which are both supported by the National Library Board. Her other works include book reviews for a blog, articles for periodicals and a school musical. For income, she does course development and training. She is married with two teenage girls who keep encouraging her to not give up writing.

Gargi Mehra lived in Oman, Singapore and New Delhi before finally settling in the IT hub of Pune, India. She enjoyed a brief stint living in Singapore's East Coast, and keeps returning to the island country that remains, in her heart, a home away from home. She currently works as a project manager with the IT arm of an international bank. Her work has appeared in numerous literary magazines online and in print, including *The Writer*, *Litro* and *On the Premises*, among others. She lives with her husband and two children.

Kalpana Mohan is a writer based in the San Francisco Bay Area. She enjoys creative writing infused with humour and heart. She is the author of *Daddykins: A Memoir of My Father and I* (2018) and *An English Made in India* (2019), and is working on her third book. Read more about her at www.kalpanamohan.com.

Clara Mok loves reminiscing about her childhood and wishes to capture snippets of Singapore's past before it disappears. She was selected for the National Arts Council Singapore's Mentor Access Project 2016–17.

Payal Morankar is a Singapore-raised Mumbai resident. She returned to her first love of writing after a detour to the world of finance. A business writer at a corporate communications agency, she is also a creative writer, Bharatanatyam dancer and avid Himalayan trekker.

Vanessa Ng Q.R. is a multidisciplinary writer who has published numerous short stories, poems, comedy scripts and more. Her short story, 'The Fat Cat Ate Dad's Hat', was adapted into an animation and screened at multiple film festivals locally and abroad.

Rolinda Onates Española is a migrant writer from Bacolod City, The Philippines. She has the author of *No Cinderella?: Poems of a Filipina Domestic Worker in Singapore, 2016–18* (2020).

Anna Onni's life goals include taming her book collection, waking up cheerful at 4 am for a twenty-one-day change-your-life challenge and joining an eco-sustainable commune. In her spare time, she is an educator who illustrates and writes in her unfinished sketchbooks. Her work can be found in *Birthday Book 20/20: Seeing Clearly* (2020) and *Food Republic: A Singapore Literary Banquet* (2020); she illustrates for The Singapore War Crimes Trials Project.

Anjali Patil grew up in India and lives in Singapore, where she is a communications professional in the financial services sector. In her spare time, she nurtures her passion for writing fiction and, to further it, attended a course at the Faber Academy in London. A graduate of the Gold Dust writer mentoring scheme, she considers herself a lifelong apprentice of the craft of fiction. She is currently working on a collection of short stories.

Ranjani Rao is a scientist by training and writer by avocation, who lives in Singapore with her family. When not working, reading or writing, she enjoys a long walk in the nature reserve near her home. She is currently working on a memoir and loves connecting with readers at www.ranjanirao.com.

Euginia Tan is a Singaporean writer who writes poetry, creative non-fiction and plays. She enjoys cross-pollinating art into multidisciplinary platforms and reviving stories. Contact her at eugtan@hotmail.com.

Audrey Tay stumbled into writing when, as a child, she realised she was happy spinning stories to fool her parents into thinking she was busy at her homework. As an adult, her writing takes place in between pandering to her pampered pooch and baking that elusive perfect cookie (chocolate chip only, please).

Phyllis Wong 'ate' books as a child. She grew up, became an accountant, morphed into a social worker/counsellor and now, she is in the 'write' time of life. She tells her stories to share the footprints God left behind in her life's journey, because she never walks alone.

Editors' Acknowledgements

We would like to thank all the contributors who submitted their stories for publication in *Singapore at Home: Life across Lines*, and to the groups that were part of the two Ungender Home events in 2018. While several of the stories were well-written in the original submission, we appreciate the contributors accepting our feedback which was aimed at making the writing shine. Pallavi especially was delighted with their unqualified acceptance of her editing, notes and additions to the text. Having publicised our call for submission through our networks of friends, colleagues and acquaintances, we also shared the call and video that we created in collaboration with Kitaab on social-media platforms, and are grateful to have received the response that we did given the pandemic situation that the world was thrust into all through 2020. And it was this very reason that spurred us on in our endeavour to create a community space through this volume, for in its pages we have found home, as we hope readers do. It has been a real pleasure corresponding with, and getting to know, the final list of twenty-one writers. And above all, we are thankful, in co-editing this anthology, for each other's understanding, wisdom, nudges, laughter and friendship in pulling through with this book through long conversations over *kopi* and *teh*—composing drafts; coordinating with our publisher and designer; selecting stories; addressing themes, choosing fonts and styles; and getting it all together.

Our publishers Zafar Anjum and Shabana Zahoor of Kitaab have been nothing but supportive. From when we approached them with the initial concept of the anthology to the book proposal that we shared with them in mid-2020, it has always been a resounding 'yes' from them. We are grateful for their encouragement and trust in our project. We are honoured, and deeply touched, by the graciousness of Alvin Pang, Cyril Wong and Felix Cheong in their prompt and enthusiastic recognition of our aims in this work. Their endorsements reinforce not only the value of our ideas as a collective but also our belief that each of our stories is significant and has an impact in the world. We would also like to thank the writing community for supporting and creating spaces for emerging artistes. Our cover designer Shikha Mehta translated Pallavi's sketch into digital art, and we thank her for her assistance. Aurelie Charmeau and Fanny Ozda held space for Pallavi as an artist; Zafar suggested she create the line drawing; and Iman was incredibly spirited in her suggestions on concept, colours and fonts.

As within, so without. Coming from India, Singapore is a second home for Pallavi, aided in great measure by friends who have given generously of their fellowship, and opened their homes and hearts for her: among others, Jérôme Buchler, Fanny Amann, Mahalia Acapandie, Chye Shu Wen, Priyanka Dhaul, Suren Rastogi, Pranav Rastogi, Cassandra Luey, Emma Louise Slattery, Leslie Guidez, Radhika Nair, Sahiba Puri and Mayank Suri. Etienne Dessaut and Nestor Guerrero Soto have been allies. Her parents Nutan and Prakash, and brother Aditya have been present for her in the making of this book, from its inception through to its publication, and she is thankful for the comfort of their presence through what has been a most trying year in human history.

Iman thanks Clara Chow for her immense support, encouragement and belief in an idea; Pallavi Narayan without whom this book could not have been possible; and Surinder Kaur and Clara Mok for wishing to extend the conversation to the wider community. As a new immigrant in Singapore well over a decade ago, she thanks the Sideek family for opening their doors and welcoming her into the family; Shameer and Shafeer for walking her through a new city; Veena and Anand, Mahesha, Nirusha, Resha, Shaffra, Shazmina, Rana and Dinusha, among others, with whom she made many memories in what was then to her a new, unfamiliar place; Sakina and Mo, Vinitha, Vivek, Krish, Weiqi, Kean, Veen Senn, Aslam, Kelly and Martin. Finally, she thanks her husband Imran, son 'Isa, brother Jaden, and parents Fahim and Najeena for their unconditional love and support.

This anthology adds to the exciting local literature that Singapore is engaged in producing and is our tribute to a place we will recall with affection as home, wherever we may go.

About the Editors

Pallavi Narayan is a PhD in Literature and holds a Diploma in Creative Writing. She has worked in academia and book publishing in Singapore and India, and has facilitated writing workshops in Southeast and South Asia throughout her career. In 2018 she was named the first Frankfurt Fellow from Singapore to the Frankfurter Buchmesse Fellowship Programme. She has presented talks, been an advisor on or moderated panels at Singapore Writers Festival, Singapore Book Council, Singapore Book Publishers Association, Singapore Art Book Fair, ASEAN India Pravasi Bharatiya Divas Writers Festival Singapore, Sing Lit Station, Asia Research Institute at National University of Singapore, and Singapore University of Technology and Design, among other forums. She has performed spoken word at Word Forward, Destination: INK and Thithikude: Tamil Open Mic in Singapore, and Red Room Taipei in Taiwan. Her short stories, poetry, articles, and book and performance reviews have been published in anthologies including *Asingbol: An Archeology of the Singaporean Poetic Form* (2017) and *SingPoWriMo 2015* and literary journals, magazines and platforms including *Kitaab, Art Republik, Passage Magazine: Friends of the Museums Singapore, We Are A Website, Jala* and Esplanade Singapore. Her watercolours and photographs have appeared in *Beyond Words Literary Magazine, Nightingale & Sparrow, Goats Milk Magazine, Analogies and Allegories Literary Magazine* and *The Lumiere Review*.

Iman Fahim Hameed has worked for over a decade in the life sciences, and has an avid interest in writing, public health and the social sciences. She received a commendation for her entry to the Royal Commonwealth Essay Competition at age ten (1997). After a long hiatus, she returned to writing with her vignettes "Colomboscapes" published on *We Are A Website* (2017). She experiments with synesthetic writing, vignettes and world Englishes to capture the dynamism of place and person. She has performed spoken word twice at Thithikudhe: Tamil Open Mic Night and created Katha, a community platform for artists to collaborate on multidisciplinary explorations. In 2018, she directed and hosted her first Katha project, a conversation on gendered spaces of the home through performative, literary and visual art. The event involved the collaboration of writers, artists and classical Indian dancers. In September 2018, she took an introductory creative writing course at LASALLE College of the Arts taught by Felix Cheong and, in 2020, her poem was featured in *UNMASKED: Reflections on Virus-time* curated by Shamini Flint. She is a trend reporter on public health issues for the UK-based charity Cov360, and is completing her Masters of Science in Public Health from the London School of Hygiene and Tropical Medicine.

For more titles from Kitaab, visit www.kitaabstore.com

Made in the USA
Las Vegas, NV
24 July 2021

26996269R00144